TRAIN TO POKIPSE

Rami

"TRAIN TO POKIPSE is a *Catcher in the Rye* for the new century and Rami Shamir is an authentic literary voice for a new lost generation. POKIPSE, much like *The Catcher in the Rye*, will be a powwow of the alienated (elite), where America's outsider youth can gather to infuse the vitality of their life for decades to come."
—**Barney Rosset**, founder of Grove Press and legendary publisher of Henry Miller, William S. Burroughs, and Samuel Beckett

"I love TRAIN TO POKIPSE."
—**Gary Indiana**, author of *The Shanghai Gesture*, *Rent Boy*, and *Do Everything in the Dark*

"Sensitivity does not come easy, but when it arrives it surrounds you entirely. When you finish this book you will be surrounded by love, sensitivity, and—hopefully—a little bit of wisdom. Live on! I did. Thank you, Rami."
—**Holly Woodlawn**, Warhol superstar and author of *A Low Life in High Heels*

"Rami Shamir is rapidly becoming the conscience of the No Generation. He is a master of that frozen moment when the eaters see what they are really eating. Gayer than Ginsberg, blacker than Kerouac, itchier than Whitman, slithering darkly toward the Billyberg Omphalos, Rami Shamir loads his pen with jizz, blood and drugs. A Nantucket sleigh ride up the rosy rectum of Generation N."
—**Phoebe Legere**, composer and performer

"Reading TRAIN TO POKIPSE is like reading Dickens. Underneath this contemporary coming of age story is the same social analysis, the same investigation of lives lived and being lived, and the same kind of empathetic heart that listens to the world and reflects it in crisp and unexpected prose. Here we find the cracked lyricism of the street, the voice of the outsider reporting on the dispossessed. Rami Shamir has a beautiful and distinctive voice and he is just starting."
—**Penny Arcade** playwright, performance artist, and author of *Bad Reputation: Performances, Essays, and Interviews*

Underground Editions
First Edition
First Printing

THIS EDITION IS LIMITED TO 911 COPIES
PRINTED ON ONE HUNDRED PERCENT RECYCLED PAPER:
216 COPIES (SIGNED) WITH A PORTRAIT OF THE AUTHOR DEFACED BY
THE AUTHOR NUMBERED FROM 1 TO 216; 400 COPIES (SIGNED) NUMBERED
FROM 217 TO 616; 295 COPIES NUMBERED FROM 617 TO 911.

Nº 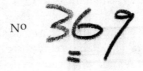 369

TRAIN TO POKIPSE

a novel by rami shamir

UNDERGROUND EDITIONS
BROOKLYN
2012

NOTICE!

As the author is hereby passing, passing, passing, he would like to take this moment to thank the following without whom TRAIN TO POKIPSE would never have been possible, and would now not be resting in your hands to (hopefully) begin its long and significant relationship with you, the Reader:

Adam Void, Jack Doroshow, David Nudo, Barney Rosset, Penny Arcade, Phoebe Legere, Holly Woodlawn, Gary Indiana, Astrid Rosset, Vanessa Edberg, Diane Bowers, Andrew H. Shirley, Shelley Wyant, Steve Dalachinsky, Yuko Otomo, his father, his sister, and his mother, Mira Shamir.

Brief excerpts from TRAIN TO POKIPSE have previously appeared, in slightly different form, in *SPANK Magazine*, *The Evergreen Review*, and *The Unbearables Big Book Of Sex*.

Cover Art and Design: Adam Void

First Printing
Underground Editions
www.undergroundeditions.com

Printed in Canada by The Prolific Group

ISBN: 978-0-615-55162-3
LCCN: 2011943272

TRAIN TO POKIPSE
by rami shamir

For the Child

"No future, no future, no future for me.
No future, no future, no future for you."

—The Sex Pistols

The bushes by the entrance gate make me anxious. The whole ride up I didn't think about anything. I just stared out the window watching the declension of civilization upon the hills, winding up the Taconic. The whole ride up I didn't think about anything, anything but you.

No one said a word in the front until we reached the sign for Red Hook, and my dad asked in broken English if this is it. I told him it is, knowing that he already knew that and was just trying to break the silence. I catch my mother's face in the rearview mirror. I wonder what she was thinking through as our tired car made its way north along the broken road. Her eyes were shining beneath their fatigue, and her face had a dead end peace about it. I don't know what the trees along the road had brought about. Maybe she noticed failure and end somewhere between the branches, up against the clear blue sky of August. Who knows? Who cares?

I have this memory of mom in a shopping mall, long ago. We were in some store (I think it was Daffy's) and my dad had gotten annoyed and wanted to go, so we're heading for the exit. My mom is walking by this pink dress that's hanging limply from the hanger. She stops and feels the fabric between her fingers, and then she gets this look on her face like things turned out way different than they were supposed to, like she was heading for Wyoming but somehow ended up in Georgia. She catches herself and puts on again the face of a loving mother and an obedient wife. She probably figured that no one noticed, that she got away unscathed by foreign eyes—but I noticed. I noticed my mother disappear into that truth we all fall into now and then; beside some pink dress in some store in New Jersey I saw it, how disappointed this woman they call my mother was with this thing they call life. Amazing, the power a pink dress can have over a woman.

Now, years later, I just caught the same look on my mother's face as she's driving with me up the Taconic to an elite college in the woods. Sometimes, I guess, the only thing the passing of the years provides us with is a new place to be unhappy; a new reminder of how much the dreaming child in us has died.

We pull up to the trailer, which is to act as my dorm for the year; and when I see Emily's dad walking toward us, my stomach begins to turn inside out. I study him to see if he notices it, the terrible shape our car is in. I study him as the car's engine shuts off to see if the scratches and the dents on the station wagon's fading grey-blue paint cut into his skin as much as they cut into mine. All I can see, though, is the blank content, forced or natural, that the comfort of privilege can pull over a person's face.

"Well, hello there," he says loudly, smiling.

"Hi Donald. Donald, this is my mom.... and Donald this is my dad."

My mom smiles. My dad takes Donald's hand and shakes it.

"I'm Meesha. I'm the dad," he says looking at the paint job on the trailer.

"So this is where they're living out the year?"

"Yeah," Donald says, still smiling. "The best money can buy, right?"

The trailers were brought in last year to replace the Ravine dorms, which are right nearby. The school's administration told us that the Ravines were falling apart; but I guess they weren't falling apart *that* bad because our summer orientation and first semester went by and all six continued to be filled to full capacity. Everyone used to say that you could tell which Ravine was the most sexually active because anytime anyone fucked in one of the rooms the whole dorm would sway. During our freshman year, I think it was the Tremblay dorm that shook the most, probably because these two kids who lived there, Jake and his girlfriend Tara, hardly went to class and spent most of their first year fucking. No one ever said anything about Hirsch shaking, where you and most of your friends lived. You guys *talked* a lot about the shaking of Tremblay but never did much shaking of your own. When we first came here, though, we were all just kids in a playground. I guess play isn't powerful enough to shake structures on the verge of condemnation.

"Emily's inside," I hear Donald say as we're unloading the boxes from the trunk. I keep looking at his eyes to see if they waver even for the briefest instant to the beat-up station wagon, to the washed-out paint, to all those dents along the doors; but all I can register is a smile that seems to be on a long sabbatical in la-la land. I'm amazed that he doesn't notice, that he actually can't *see* this wreck on wheels. The large piece of metal swinging in the air as we unload the boxes from the trunk makes it even more obvious, this poverty of ours. I feel it has to draw attention to everything else—the dirty clothes my dad is wearing, my mom's obvious attempt at looking middle-class, but—nothing. Donald sees absolutely nothing.

My mom decides that she wants to walk around, take a look at the campus and all. The whole time she keeps putting her arm around me, and the whole time I'm tensing up, like she's some kind of secret that refuses to be kept hidden.

We're in Blithewood Garden. My mom's reclining on the grassy hill. The garden is below, at the bottom of the hill; Blithewood Mansion, where the Economics School is housed, lies behind us; and before us is the Hudson River, cut in its center by a stretch of land on which are built the train tracks. In the summer you and I would sit here and watch the sun set itself to sleep behind the blue mountains lying beyond the western shore.

Sometimes we'd be there as the silver line of a southbound train would cut through the twilight like an uninterrupted thought. Sometimes we'd be there in our shorts and loose t-shirts at that moment when the Universe seeks to migrate its light to another source. We'd watch as the rays went from the sun to the train cutting across the river and then that light would hit us, turning the ephemeral possibilities of the air into flesh, blood, and cum—into two boys kissing on the privileged hills of some American college nestled in the woodwork.

"This," I hear my mom say, "feels like a vacation." She's looking at me and her face is all lit up—and I see across all the crap that's happened between this moment and that one, back across all the moments of beauty and filth, which are piled one on top of the other like the stretched-out skin of an overused cunt; and I think how every moment in a life is like its own Universe; I think how every moment in a life is filled with the full intensity of a million stars dying and a million stars being born; and how every moment in a life has an immeasurable amount of black emptiness between all that birth and all that death. Every moment in every life has this much potential, so imagine—how powerful is the human life being built on countless of these things called moments.

I see the green eyes of my mother; and she looks like that little girl in the black and white picture that sits by her bedside and has throughout all the apartments she's lived in in New York. She looks so innocent in that picture. She looks like nothing ever happened yet.

And now those same green eyes are capturing the look that's on my face. They see that I just want them to disappear and take her with them. They see that I just want her to go far away, back down to Brooklyn, so that I can rush over and see you, rush over and get back to a happier pretense of myself.

"All right," she sighs, beginning to pick her body off the ground. "Let's leave him alone."

"Why?" my dad asks cruelly. "We just got here."

"Because," my mom says, already heading up the hill, "our son wants us to leave."

No I don't. No, I meant to say it, I don't, but instead I just follow her up the hill, and the three of us silently walk back to that grey-blue station wagon, which, when I see it, looks more faded and beat-up than when we had left. She takes one last look around. My mother. My beautiful mother.

"If you need anything, call," she says, hugging me really hard. I feel those two uprooted arms around me, and I know that she means it with everything she's got left. I watch as the car pulls away, and I see tears in her green eyes. They aren't looking at me, though, or at anything around me. Instead, they seem focused on some point in time that probably never existed beyond the county limits of my mother's dreams. And then she disappears. My mom. My beautiful mom.

I hear Nancy, Donald's ex-wife, yelling from the kitchen. She's asking if I want any of the cookies she brought up with her from Long Island. I hold it back, my anger and my sadness and my self-hatred. I just swallow it down and try to forget about that little girl driving down the Taconic to her lonely reality of disappointments.

Swallow it down. Swallow it all the way down. That's a good boy.

The sick thing is that by the time I see your house from Annandale Road, I do forget. By then the grey-blue car must have just been nearing the first exit signs for Poughkeepsie, leaving another hour and a half for my mom to stare out at the trees and bite her lip to keep from letting my dad see her cry. I wonder how long she held it in.

A t your house. The cars spill out from the driveway into the street.

The house you and your friends rented that year was the only one on campus not already owned by faculty. It was high on a hill and right off where Annandale Road curved into the north, concluding part of the campus. Later on, when it became a main social area for the school's student body, people would refer to it as "The Barn," or "The House," or a lot of the time as "_____*'s House." It was never anybody else's—that's how much the world adored you.

I recognize some of your friends as I'm going up the back porch, which leads into your kitchen. They've tapped a keg. Unknown freshman girls surround them trying out different lines to get into the bed of the upper class. When I step into your kitchen, I see you right away.

You're in the center of the room, and all these kids are standing around you, fixated on everything you do. I stand at a distance and watch you; thinking about how the only thing I ever wanted is standing there in the same room. So close. You raise your head, and the ceiling light hits your eyes and makes them blue. You see me: and all at once become real, too real. You're the prettiest boy I will ever see.

I'm crossing the floor of your kitchen, but I feel like I'm crossing the Hudson itself. I'm almost there, at your feet, between your shoulder blades, where I like to rest my head—the spot you always told me was the safest place on Earth. Up against you, with your long arms around me, I can feel the pulsation of your cock as it pushes sporadically through your jeans against my belly. I can't shake the feeling, though, that I'm still there—in the middle of your kitchen floor, stuck in the middle of the Hudson and getting nowhere. For some reason, it feels like I'm drowning. I see the bright lights of that safe harbor across the shore begin to fade. Our bodies are together, but someone isn't here. Is it you? Is it me? Maybe it's the both of us.

"Let's go upstairs," I say, pushing that frightening sensation away. In your room (the one you loved so much, but that Maggie called first and that I told you to take for yourself anyway because you deserve anything you want), we exchange presents. You give me a Lou Reed CD, remembering how at the end of last year, when we first met, I used to love when you'd sing "Pale Blue

Eyes" to lull me to sleep. I give you a hymn book from the nineteen-thirties that I bought in a Port Jeff. thrift shop. On the first page someone has scribbled in black ink, "Charles Lucky was hanged in Brockville Feb. 16th 1893."

We sit on the edge of your bed and stare into the blue of the other's eyes. It feels like falling through an icy lake and finding a better definition for Heaven. Pay attention. Here's a moment never to reoccur until our own separate times diminish. In the final moment of a life, all the moments that made it what it was come together, arriving one on top of the other like station signs seen through the window of a speeding train. Until then, this moment will never reoccur; so, pay attention. Watch as my pink lips go for yours, your pink lips for mine. Watch as these two pairs of young lips tremble on the periphery of something unexplainable, tremble in the massive electricity of youth, which is always present in the diminishing border surrounding the nearing lips of two boys in love, one with the other. These are the only kisses I ever gave away willingly. The rest—the fucking in New York City backrooms, the wooing of familiar strangers into new but recognizable beds, the piss, the shit, the cum, but especially the kisses—were all just notes in the requiem of your loss. I guess I didn't pay attention.

Later on in the day, you come with me and my roommates to pick out a puppy for the trailer. We haven't really said that much all day, not with words at least; and now that our bodies have been satisfied, our minds seek out verbal language on some shopkeeper's stoop in Red Hook. I ask you if everything's 0K, but you stay silent and keep staring at the sidewalk.

"Whatever it is, we'll get through it," I say, but you just keep staring at that sidewalk. I get scared that maybe you're thinking of slipping down that very sidewalk onto the street and taking a walk. I know if that happens I'll never catch up with you—your legs are way too long. So I wrap myself underneath your arms, but something there isn't right. It's like the summer air is moving away in a slow languish into the irretrievable past. You look at me: and for a moment I see heartbreak.

"Something doesn't feel right," you say.

It's hot outside. My boyfriend's beautiful.

"I know—but it's probably just the change of it all. A week ago this was all ours. Now we have to share it with the world."

Swallow it down. Swallow it all the way down. That's a good boy.

At night we lie next to each other in your bed. We're shirtless and in our boxers. The window's open to let in the summer air. I go down to give you head. I gratefully swallow your cum. After a long time making out, you get hard. I go down to give you head again. When we wake up in the morning, you're feeling better.

See, it was just the change of it all. Things always get better. Always.

I passed away most of that summer dreaming of you. Sometimes we'd spend three hours on the phone saying nothing but "I love you." We were simply happy to hear each other breathe. Just to hear the breath of the boy you loved was everything.

I worked for two weeks at TGI Fridays in Times Square; and then, one day, on a whim, I took the train to Poughkeepsie, and you picked me up. I'm exiting the train station, and I see you leaning against your brother's SUV, looking slightly uncomfortable in your blue jeans: all of you is focused on the entrance; all of you is wound up for all of me. I stayed for a week. We tried to accomplish our long put-off goal of losing "it" to each other, but only got there a fraction of the way. I couldn't get my cock inside you for the nerves, and anyway, we both knew that's not how it ought to be. When you entered me (I can still feel how hard and fresh you were, still feel you underneath all that skin which now is dying), I felt complete. I didn't let you advance, though, because I got scared of bleeding from my ass and then having to go to the hospital where you would learn I had no health insurance and you'd see that poverty I was trying to hide so stop, stop, please—I'm sorry. What's wrong, did I hurt you? No, that was perfect. It was? Yeah, I'm just nervous—I love you. I love you too.

We'd try again, but wouldn't fuck completely until about two weeks before it ended. Then we fucked all the time. There were days we fucked seven, eight times. I couldn't get enough and neither could you, but the best of it was that you came inside me every time. The first time you had asked for my permission, but after that you just followed what was natural. You just rode on the notes of my yelling and the balls hitting the ass and your lungs gasping and the nineteen-year-old cock rising from your hips going in and out of my nineteen-year-old ass pushing back and forth and those hidden silent tones as your eyes stared down into mine and mine stared up back into yours and I could see a hazy outline of other things like the ceiling light behind your head and the curves and lines of the rest of the room but everything is formless that isn't those two eyes because I'm fully there riding it with you, riding all the notes of our love. I still remember looking away after we just finished our inauguration into manhood. Your warm body's next to mine; you're breathing heavily. The red numbers on your digital clock announce that it's 8:46 AM.

Later on, when I'd be on my ass shitting air into the toilet bowl, some cum would spill out, slightly darkened by the journey. I'd get up and watch it float around in the toilet water, my boxers wrinkled at my feet. I'd stand there thinking how this was the end result not only of the hours on your bed, but the hours in my head and yours—the seconds of looking across crowded tables at each other and waiting by classroom doorways for the lesson to end added up. This—your ejaculated cum expelled from my insides into Dutchess County water— was everything you and I were, expressed concisely in earthly terms. This homosexual misbirth floating around

12

in the toilet bowl was a sort of child, our child, and I looked at it with love.

That week I saw Kate Weiss. She had moved to Hudson and drove me my first time into that lonely upstate town. We ate at some vegan restaurant and talked about our boyfriends. One day, I decided that I needed to go back to New York. Immediately. I simply got too scared of it all. For some reason, Hudson made me feel that things end, that they die, and I got frightened. You drove me to the train station, and after you parked I just sat in the passenger seat and cried.

As the train pulled away, I saw you leaning against a pole on the platform. I couldn't read you, but I could tell that all of you still loved me. Maybe you were sad to see me go without a reason. Maybe I got you scared. I wouldn't come back until my parents drove me up in that grey-blue car, winding up the Taconic, at the beginning of the school year.

I see you. I see you in the light of summer's setting sun. The wind is thinking troubled thoughts but succors her limbs to silence. There comes a time when all things end and these will end as all things do. But still. I see you. You raise your hand looking right at me with an empty face.

And then you're gone.

Davidand I are on the L train going into the city. I'm standing on the edge. He's telling me I should stop doing coke if it makes me unhappy, but I'm not listening to anything he's saying because he's high too, and the lights are really bright, and I feel like the sunglasses make me look suspicious, so I keep taking them off, holding them for a bit, and putting them back on. David just kicked a bad heroin addiction, and he claims he hasn't done anything since—"not *even* coke," but that I have a way of bringing that side out so he really "didn't have a choice." He's telling me about some new boy he's in love with, and I just sit back staring through my sunglasses at the receding tunnel lights, feeling like everything is dead.

When we get to the Cock we decide to walk around for a bit and smoke a cigarette so we can cool off from the train ride. I hate the Cock, he says. Me too, but what else is there to do? He agrees, so we walk in, get a drink, get on line for the bathroom, and then sit on the couch, high and silent until last call, checking out the crowded bar for something that'll make us happy. Nothing comes. We separate and go different ways, both heading toward a substitute for home.

No one's on the beach at Coney Island, and the Ferris wheel, though vacant and closed, can't help but be moved by the winds. When I was a kid I got a splinter walking barefoot down the boardwalk with my dad, who in those days was really tall. Looking at the ocean from the platform I sense that this is where New York disappears, sloping gently into endless unformed chaotic water.

I'm sitting in the corner of Opaline's VIP room. The whole place is empty except for three DJs, two bartenders, and Jack, who's jacked up on pills and tina, dancing away the emptiness on a makeshift stage. I watch him wondering where he is right now. Max's Kansas City? Studio 54? Jackie 60? Wherever he is he sure isn't here. That would be a waste of drugs.

I wish I had something to run away to, but the coke just numbs that nostalgia for something I never had. It does that for most kids my age. I guess that's why most of us spend most of our time getting high.

The three DJs keep playing "Rocket Queen" over and over, really punching the point to the empty room.

"Here I am. And you're a Rocket Queen. I might be a little young but honey I ain't naive."

I kiss Brandon on my way out, and turn right on Fifth Ave, walk to West 33rd St, then west to Seventh. On Seventh Ave, I turn back around, uptown. The platform on 42 Street is filled with people waiting for the train. Some jock keeps giving me dirty looks, probably because my pubic hair is hanging out of my low riders. He's not very cute, and he's wearing a wrinkled polo shirt with sandals and shorts, which all makes him look even less attractive. I have this vision of tying him up to a bedpost and taking a piss on his face, then cutting his face with a single edge razor blade.

Walking up 5 AV I see a banner tied tightly to a street lamp. On the banner, the New York skyline's black, set against a red background. Above the skyline are the words, "N.Y.C. & COMPANY, ARTS AND CULTURE." I look around the empty streets of Friday night, then at the tattoo on my arm: the skyline buildings are in black too; but there's this zigzagging line that violently crosses them out, like graffiti. Except the zigzagging line across my upper arm *isn't* graffiti. It's more like a graffiti inversion, a graffiti of gentrification, a yuppie's tag, and it's crossing out my city, our city, the real New York. Break a window, and art is born. Fix the broken window, and art begins to die.

I laugh thinking about it all, about how wide that chasm is between how you're told it is and how it really is: A distance as great as that from Opaline to Jackie 60 or Studio 54 or Max's Kansas City. A distance no train can cover without running over a life in the process.

MADR, SerF, WAKE UP AND SMELL THE MISERY, Avenue U, CHiP.MOD, DAES, PAX, MUTZ, Kings Highway, neST, SOneR, BaaL, Bay Parkway, CHEF, Kn, MADR, CHiP.MOD, TUSK 05, 20 Avenue, ..IN MEMORY.OF.CRAZ.. THE ACID 36 MOB.., BRUZ, ZU, WH.SCEE, MADR, MUTZ, SeZR, DUNE, Fort Hamilton Parkway,...

I'm sitting outside with Melvin at Republic. I'm drinking a ginger mojito, and he's having a raspberry lemonade with *"some* kind of alcohol in it." He doesn't know what kind, and he doesn't care. "As long as it tastes good and feels fine, who cares?" Halfway through his drink he's trashed, and toward the end of mine I'm trashed too. We've been at the Russian-Turkish Baths all day, so our bodies are cleansed; and anyway, we're not used to drinking anything besides water without at least a *couple* of lines.

We light our cigarettes together, mirroring thoughtlessly accepted rituals, and right away the waitress comes out and apologizes, but evidently *"it's illegal"* to smoke at our table. We get up and walk ten feet. Melvin says, "Big difference this makes," as all the smoke blows south toward the tables. "No difference, except that it makes us uncomfortable. But you know how it is," I say, taking a long drag off my Camel Light, "Light a cigarette, and somewhere in the city some withered cunt of a bitch yuppie will put her nose up in the air and scream like we're setting the whole place on fire." She senses it—unclean behavior, *threatening* behavior.... "How can *anyone* smoke? How can *anyone* do something outside of what *I* think is acceptable?" The angry thought rushes through the mind of this caricature, who is sadly real, too real, and she runs outside and makes a phone call to 311, that her outrage may be forever noted in the chronicles of Man. Then she goes and has some wine over dinner, "just one glass or maybe two," at some restaurant downtown, where she mourns the dwindling rights under this conservative government with her colleague.

Three bottles of Sonoma Valley Pinot Noir later:

"What *are* you going to do tonight, Charlene?"

"I have to have those proofs ready for the PC *Mein Kempf* by tomorrow morning."

Charlene leers at the young waiter passing by the table. *Isn't that he, coming to me, n*—o!..: "Waiter! Waiter! Wai!-*ter*! Pinot Noir please sometime today!" she yells, shaking the glass in her right hand and sanctifying the table in a purple shower of Sonoma Valley.

She turns—"And you, what are *you* going to do, Marlene?"

"I'm going to walk my yuppie puppy; (but if no one's looking, I won't pick up any of the pooh!)"

The waiter comes.

He places the glass's base on top of the check's corner.

Charlene and Marlene stare at it, look into one another's eyes: "No man *here*.... we could always…"

Two hours later, a young yuppie recently transplanted from the Great Plains and promoted to INSERT USELESS COMPANY POSITION AND CORPORATE TITLE HERE at INSERT USELESS CORPORATE MEDIA OR PUBLISHING ENTITY HERE is dialing 3-1-1…. *ring… ring…* "Yes, Mister Mayor Police, there are two old lesbians in the building across from me who've left their window ·open, and the things they're doing to that Saint Bernard!... something involving a Nazi flag, a noose, and a bottle of… red wine…"

After Republic, we decide we're tired of being outside in the daylight, so we head uptown to Jack's. When we get out at FIFTH AVE., I get a Coke, and Melvin gets a hot dog. He's wearing jean short-shorts that come right up to the bottom of his butt cheeks. All the men on 5 AV stop and turn to watch these two boys in their sunglasses walk the tree-lined street. "Girl," Melvin laughs, "these men are *feeling* it."

Melvin and Jack are going to Happy Valley, and Matthew thinks he "*might* go," but he doesn't know, because even though Jack tells him they'll get in for free, and Melvin assures him that there will be a couple of bottles at Amanda's table, Matthew keeps saying, "I know, but I really don't have the cash to spend, and you know how it is," and Melvin replies he does with a smile and a laugh and a look. Sam's there too, and he's going to go for sure because as goes the majority so goes Sam. I imagine him lying awake at night in bed wondering how many people are asleep and how many are out, stressing over the right decision to make. He'd count sheep, but then he might find his face cut and pasted on their imaginary bodies; and how could he be among the sheep when he's going to write the Great American Novel? I told him he's a sheep one time and he ba-ba'd that I'm a junky. I imagine that *novel* he's working on: "The Collected Misreadings of a Sensitive Homosexual in an Undergrad Lit. Class." I imagine the praise for this fine

19

young man chorusing out from a menagerie of critical circles: "This Sensitive Sam is the new literary genius of our times.... his interpretation of canonical verse is timely and long overdue—'Good neighbors make fences, where are there cows?' indeed! BRAVO, BRAVA, if this were a film I'd use both my thumbs—(literary wink across the table). Yes, I agree—O 'Do not go gentle in at night wild men be gay and you my father I pray do not go gentle in.' O yes! Sensitive Sam knows what we all feel, from Dylan Thomas to this seasoned geriatric critic. O yes! Mr. Sam knows that we all feel like making love— *to daddy*!" And Sam's just standing there the whole time, obedient as a puppet on Risperdol, as he accepts the praise—("We'll start you on Risperdal immediately.... conservative approach... 16mgs a day... as with all such things there are some side-effects.... but the quality of life is what's important here, the quality of your life."), smiling at his victory over *her*: BINGO MOM, I'm no retard—dysleksia has me well served!

· I'm not going out with them because everyone in the room is getting on my nerves. I get up and go lie down in Jack's bed. I take a Marinol and put "Siamese Dream" into the CD player. In twenty minutes, I've disappeared, flowing with the music, back in time, past Williamsburg and Bard to high school, and I see all of us as one—from Boston through New York and Philadelphia and Baltimore into Richmond and Asheville through Houston and Denver into Oakland and Portland—before we got let down, before we came of age into nothing.

It was just this last Sunday—or was it the Sunday before that? It's hard to remember anything when your life's become a hangover. Wait, it was Saturday, this past Saturday, that we all went to the Bank. It's now officially called "Element," but before that, in its heyday, the club was called "The Bank."

It's too bad they changed the name because what are New York clubs these days but their own types of banks—places where people go to invest, transfer, and cash in on the capital available to them. The pretty boys and girls use their looks as capital; the known names use their fame; and the yuppies, having nothing but the shallowest of things available for their disposal, use cold-hard-cash or razor-thin-plastic. It's a regular fucking whorehouse these days in the clubs of New York City—sell yourself for whatever you can get, and then wake up in the morning and go to work to sell yourself a little more.

The club has reserved an alcove away from the dance floor where everyone is gathering. I'm really thankful there's a place to sit away from the crowd. As an added bonus, it's right by the bathrooms. In half an hour, it seems like the whole place is full: the bottom floor where the dance floor is, the balcony where the go-go boys are, and the alcove where we're all sitting. The line for the bathroom never gets too long, so you can tell the place isn't really a coke place, at least not like the Cock. I spend most of the night drinking champagne and having pointless conversations.

I can tell that a lot of the kids around me are sneaking off to the bathrooms. I didn't call my dealer earlier because I'm trying to quit again; but now I'm really drunk, so I start asking around for a dealer.

Jay calls me over and introduces me to B(*crackle*)a. I can't hear her name because it's so loud, so I ask again. Still unable to make it out I ASK AGAIN. She sighs and looks right into my eyes and says, loudly, dramatically, hoping everyone can hear her, "Fasten your seatbelts— it's going to be a bu*mpy* night! For the last time it's B-AhN-Ka." I have a deep urge to tell B-AhN-Ka that she still looks like a man, a deeper urge to take her in the bathroom and flush her made-up face in the toilet for the remainder of the night, but I know she's my best chance at scoring coke this late, so I remain silent.

Of course, she rips me off on the bag, the bitch. It's not that she gave me shit. The coke was coke. It's just that she gave me way less than what I paid for. Upon seeing the bag, my earlier urge to flush her face in the toilet transforms into a bloody scene where I'm cutting off her trannie tits and feeding them to her; but I'm in the stall with Melvin and Jack already, and after we do the whole bag ("that fucking cunt, can you believe it, the *whole* bag was three lines") I don't care anymore. As we're leaving the club, Bianca's standing outside, smoking. I step on her foot *hard* when I pass her, and I can hear her yelling "FUCKHead" as I get in the cab. I'm laughing as Melvin gives the driver directions to Greenroom.

"If there's any place that will be full of dealers at four

in the morning it's the Greenroom," I tell him, as the buildings mix into wavy lines and lights outside the taxi window.

"Yeah," he says. "Anyway, girl, it's the only place we can go where we won't have to pay, and where we can stay all night and get higher...."

"...And higher..."

"...And higher. That's right, girl," he says, laughing.

Higher and higher and higher. One way or the other it's the ultimate goal of everyone I know. Always keep getting higher because this here, right now, just isn't enough.

We get to Greenroom and sit around drinking crappy drinks for a bit. The club remains empty, and we begin to get nervous. Soon our panic subsides: we find a dealer. He tries to sell me a small bag for forty bucks; I tell him I won't give him any more than twenty-five; he agrees. Melvin and I head down the long stairs and turn into one of the three bathrooms, which are right by the doorway.

Now we're upstairs sitting on the couch by the bar and I feel it, that numbness setting in and taking me far away to some place I'd rather be. I see the headlights of the train creeping toward me. I can't wait to get out of here.

A boy comes and sits down next to me with some girl who turns out to be his cousin. We talk for a while, and he's getting me hard just by the way he's looking at me. I can tell he just can't wait to fuck the hell right out of me. This guy I know—Paul or Joe or Peter or something—

who I sent out to find me a good dealer, comes and tells me that he's found the guy.

"You like coke?" I ask the boy.

"I *love* coke."

The boy and I go downstairs to the bathroom, and I buy this large bag from some black guy for seventy bucks. He wants eighty, but I tell him I only have seventy—so he agrees. He doesn't have a choice because the place isn't that packed. An empty after-hours is a dealer's nightmare and a cokehead's dream. The boy also buys a bag, and then the dealer leaves with whatever his name is who found me the drugs. On our fifth keyful of coke, I tell the boy that I think he's hot. He says, "Yeah? Good, 'cause I can't wait to fuck you."

I smile, "Oh really, well I hope you like submissive boys."

I begin to rub his hard cock through his jeans.

"There's no better ass to fuck," he says, "than an ass that's begging to be fucked."

He pushes me against the wall and starts kissing me. In seconds, I have my palm wrapped around the large thick cock protruding from his open zipper. We decide to go to his hotel room. "All I have to do is ask my cousin. I haven't seen her for a while, and I don't want her to be upset."

"Fine. Go do that. I'm going to find my friend."

He leaves the bathroom, and I lay out three lines and then, inhale, one, inhale, by one, inhale, by one. When I get upstairs I see that boy on that same couch by the bar arguing with his cousin. Melvin isn't there, so I turn the corner to see if he's in the next room, and then I see him sitting there with Josh.

I used to be really close with Josh. For a moment in the New York night it was always me and him, sometimes against the world. But then something happened. He found a boyfriend. I fell apart. Then *he* fell apart. Maybe I had left him one too many times, coked up out of my mind, to go fuck some kid I could care less than a shit about in the morning. Maybe he berated me one too many times in public. Or maybe it was just that time finally caught up with our rocky relationship and turned it into dust. Who knows, who cares? Besides the basic social acknowledgments, Josh and I barely say a word to one another. The communication has been whittled down to looks—playful looks, accusatory looks, indefinable looks—always through coked-up eyes, and always across tables covered in stale liquor glasses and cigarette boxes of varying brands. When River, his boyfriend, walks in (as he just did), even that stops. Next to romance, what's the use of friendship? For me and Josh, friendship's just a final option.

(I wonder if it's normal to care so little where once you cared so much.)

The boy comes with his cousin and sits next to me. I try to get him to leave immediately because we both have coke, we're both horny as hell, but mostly because being around Josh at some dumb after-hours on Sunday morning makes me feel all the things I hate to feel. It makes me feel like no one ever sticks around; like either you're walking away, or they're walking away, but that always *someone's* walking away. It makes me remember how much battling with love is like battling with coke. Mostly, though, it makes me remember that all dances end, that all nights end, and that all life ends. Life is ending as I think these very thoughts.

Melvin tells me they're going to some exclusive party. I tell him I don't care because I'm going back with this boy to his hotel room. "Does he know that you're a bottom?" Melvin asks. "Why?" I ask. ""Look at him, girl—he looks pretty bottomish to me," Melvin says. "Yeah, he knows I'm a bottom, and he's totally fucking into it." And then it happens.

Just as likely as a high can turn nasty, so can a night. Usually they go hand in hand. The trick is, never expect anything so you'll never be disappointed. But when your blood is being boiled over into another dimension by that white innocence they call coke, all you *can* do *is* expect; all you *can* do *is* want. Cocaine requires that you desire. Cocaine requires that you dream. And since all we want, all we dream is to be alive, we look from our dead present and try to recreate the living past, that great time of which most of us have heard, and some of us have even lived. The time of endless nightlife, endless art, endless *danger* everywhere. I've been told that if you keep riding *that* train, that train cocaine, you'll keep hitting a brick wall. Who cares? These days, it's dreaming that's the most dangerous thing because everyone's scared that one day you might smash right through that brick wall and tear the world apart.

(I just hit the brick wall, though, and I didn't go through it.)

The boy tells me we can't go home together. He really wants to, I can tell he does, but he can't. "Why?" He tries to feed me some crap, but I can tell that it's his cousin. She claims it's "logistically" not possible. She's high as a kite, and I figure she just doesn't want to lose his coke to me; and knowing the power of the drug, and knowing that I have to keep up my appearance, I say, "That's too bad, but if you have to go I think you should go now." He asks for my number. I tell him it's pointless to have my number because I just wanted to fuck him tonight. "Honestly, I don't need to know you. You just looked like a good fuck." I wasn't being cruel; for me romance doesn't last beyond the night or beyond the final line.

I turn to Melvin and ask if I can go with them to the party. He says he doesn't know, that he has to ask Josh, that the guest list is "limited." Then they all disappear without even saying good-bye. Now it's just me and Chris, this bald-headed Jamaican who deals.

Across the room are two boy couples. One of them has his shirt off, and each one keeps indiscriminately switching which one of the four heads he's sticking his long tongue into. Some kid plops down next to me, and he looks really fucked up, so I ask him if he's OK, and he tells me he is; he just hates it that no one will dance with him.

"Do you want to dance?" he asks.

"No, I don't want to dance."

He lets out a tired sigh, then springs up onto his lonely dance floor. I see Chris looking around and figure he's still waiting for the boys.

"What are you waiting for?" I ask him.

"For Josh to come back so we can go to the party."

"Don't waste your time. They left," I tell him, watching the lonely boy move across the dance floor.

"Didn't they just go downstairs to the bathrooms?"

"No. They left, without you and without me."

All of a sudden, for no reason at all, Chris starts to laugh, and the way his smile stretches out beyond his face into the room, I can tell that I am falling. I am falling. I am falling. I begin to notice that the shirtless boy is giving me this cold stare from across the room as the others are making out by his exposed cock.

"What time is it?" I ask Melvin, no wait, that's Chris.

"Eight forty-six. They close in seventeen minutes."

The lonely boy keeps moving across the dance floor.

I look toward the boys across the room, and all four of them are now staring right at me with this cold look that's making me feel numb everywhere, like my flesh is becoming stone. Their hands are moving along each other's cocks, intertwining, hands and cocks, like a thousand fornicating snakes, and they keep staring right at me as if their eyes are detached from the rest of their bodies.

"Chris." I manage to say through the lump in my throat.

"Yeeeeeah?..." "Eeaaah?..." "Eaah?..."

"Hey, Chris." I say again, breaking away from their stare. "Do you wa—wanna give me a bump? I—I ran out."

"Sure man. Meet me downstairs."

He goes first; I follow him a little bit after—down the long staircase.

When I get downstairs, Chris is waiting by the stalls, though two bathrooms are open.

"Why aren't we going in?" I ask him.

"Hold on, I want to watch this," he tells me, and then I see what it is he wants to watch.

The doors to the bathrooms are made of tinted glass.

I see two shadows through the glass.

The two shadows are fucking.

There's a black outline of some boy bent over, and that outline is pushing back and forth against another black outline of a different boy who's standing straight up and has one of his arms wrapped around the bent boy's torso. Then the standing kid kind of curves his body low, and I can see him begin to thrust his hips really hard, back-and-forth, as he uses his arm to pull the kid that's bent over up closer into him. Close into his hips to where his cock begins. I can see the hips of the standing shadow move really fast like they're hoping that if they move fast enough they might reach the speed of light and become visible. But all that happens is that this kid on the bottom gets fucked harder and harder and you can hear him moan, a moan beyond pain, a moan beyond help, a moan that, after it keeps emanating with each ever-shortening thrust over and over again, begins to sound like a death rattle. Then I hear slapping as the standing kid pulls the bent-over shadow up by the hair. Then I hear someone say, "You keep moaning you fucking bitch, keep-" (grunt) "moan-" (grunt) "ing-" (grunt) "for-my—Fucking!—Cock!"

MoooOOOoooan!

"Chris."

"MooOOOooan."

"Chris!"

Moooaaaaan.

All I can see are the stairs as I race up them really fast, two-by-two, and then the grey sky, the grey sky that's shrouding the death of another night.

I pass some lady pushing a stroller. She looks horrified. I realize that I haven't checked my nose once tonight. I rush to the rearview mirror of some car and bend my face down to see that both my nostrils and my upper lip are crusted with white powder. I begin to frantically wipe it off with my shirt, and then I feel like I have to get out of there right away. I hail a cab and get into the back seat.

I sit in the back seat not knowing where I am or who I am. I'm completely empty, and my heart is beating like it's about to pop, pop, pop.

"Hell-*oo*. How many times do I have to ask you?" I hear someone say.

It's the driver.

"Where are you heading?"
Right now, I'm heading to the very bottom.
"I don't know," I hear someone say.
It's me.
"Take me anywhere. Anywhere but here."

8 Avenue, SOUTHERN 139823, SOUTHERN 139838 dark dark dark light dark lightlight dark light dark dark dark dark, TRAVEL THROUGH HISTORY, TURN YOUR DREAMS INTO REALITY NYSCAS New York School of Career and Applied Studies, Planned Service Changes NR NIGHTS Uptown trains stop at the express track, *DeKALB, Ill.—Steve Kazmierczak, the man who walked silently into a classroom here on Thursday and opened fire, was not seen as struggling in college. He was not an outcast. And until recently, at least, he was not seen as brooding,* dark darkdarkdarkdarkligggght, 59 Street,...

Somewhere in my life the snow is falling. I'm walking slowly across the frozen lake with Emily. The lake is by the arboretum on the outskirts of Port Jeff. We haven't said anything for a couple of seconds or minutes or days. I look up at the sky and see a stork flying through the snowfall, and I remember Smith Point. Hey Em, remember when we used to go to the beach at Smith Point in the summer? We'd try to wake up early but would usually just sleep in until your mom

31

came and warned us to get up before we missed the day. We'd get in your car and make our usual stop at that deli right outside of Port Jeff. where we'd get sandwiches, bottles of water, and huge iced teas with lemonade mixed in.

Remember that one time at the beach when the storks came down and attacked the picnic? There was that one bird that kept going for the bread bag with his beak, pushed by a motion that wasn't motivated just by persistence. It was jagged, it was swift, like he knew, like that bird knew, he better do what he has to do, and he better do it fast. It was persistence under the influence of anxiety; and remember how we just couldn't wait for the family to get back from the water, and when they came back, remember how pissed off the dad was, and how the little girl, I start to laugh, how the little girl was like, "daddy the birdies ate all the bread," and that just got him so fucking mad that he started to chase that one lonely stork—I stop to catch my breath—yelling up at the sky, "You fucking asshole. I'll kill you! I'll kill you! I'LL FUCKING KILL YOU!" and the little girl started to cry, and we just stared at each other trying our best not to laugh.

I look over to Emily to see if she remembers, but I can't tell because she just keeps staring down at the ground. The covered sun is changing everything from a heavy black to a heavier grey as it rises in the air. On the western shore I can see the houses I used to admire in the summer disappearing into another world. Pieces of them disintegrate, their porches disintegrate, their floor-to-ceiling windows vanish into the air, but some objects escape the local massacre of the littoral winter and remain clear and distinct.

The snow is falling against the light hairs of Emily's neck. Her head's being pushed to the ground, seemingly by the force of the snowfall, like the insignificant flakes of frozen water have gained the strength of battering rams made for the walls of medieval towers. I begin to wonder if even the gentle forces of the world have become too much for her to bear.

We walk on the frozen lake for a while, and then she finally says, "I hate my heart." Nothing about the birds. Nothing about the picnic. It's like she didn't even hear me. Maybe she doesn't remember the story of the hungry stork, or maybe the telling wasn't strong enough to make her forget the story of herself, the story of Emily, the story of a girl searching around in a frozen world. Remembering is one thing; forgetting is another. We're all too greedy, too scared to let all the shit of life go, because what would we be if we forgot the past? Something new, something just born, or something about to die, but always something on the periphery of freedom. To forget about the past is to threaten yourself with freedom, and it takes a really good storyteller to make a person accept the threat.

"I really, I really hate my heart," she says, still looking to the ground.

I look back up at the sky hoping to see that stork again, but instead I get this sensation like I'm not myself alone. I get this feeling of commotion within, like there are thousands of people inside of me who are frozen in ice and trying to claw out. I see them vaguely from an aerial vantage point, from the perspective of someone who's looking down, someone who's beyond it all, and I see that the cold has purpled their limbs and bruised their extremities to a darkness close to frozen mud. I can feel the nails breaking against the solid ice as these desperate prisoners frantically scratch the walls of their cells. I can hear their mouths expel pleas for help, pleas coming out not as intended screams but as impotent expirations of air heated to the temperature of a star's interior.

I try to fade away, try to push that feeling back down, but it's nine in the morning, and all around me is an unusable whiteness, so I have to stay here, stay here and feel that clawing from the inside being waked by that crying from the outside. I have to stay and suffer this valvular earthquake on a frozen lake somewhere in the eastern suburbs of Long Island.

"I really hate my heart," Emily says again, "and I don't know what to do about it."

I search my pockets and find a bag, but it's empty, so I drop it on the lake. I look back up at the sky. The hidden sun remains low, and the world remains stuck between the boundaries of bleak colors. The pale sky is spread out above us like a body that's been placed upon the slab. It remains still for a long time, but when the hidden beams of the rising sun break across it weakly, the sky moves violently—the way a creature would if struck by a compact blow. My head hurts, we haven't slept all night, and the coke is wearing off. I keep looking up at that body on its stratospheric slab, and I begin to wonder if the snow falling isn't actually just pieces of that body being hacked away by some unseen force. Maybe Emily's neck hasn't been weakened. Maybe where I see snowfall Emily's aware enough to feel the severed limbs of once important things crashing to the ground. Maybe her heart is still very much alive; and in the language of the dying, maybe life is just a concise synonym for weakness.

"What am I going to do about her?" she asks me. Her, her, her. Her is a girl named Lisa; but before Lisa had come along, her was a girl named Katrina; and before Katrina showed up, her was a girl named Stephie, and Jane, and Susie—and Rachel and Dakota and Nicole. Her is a ghost phantom that travels from body to body, always promising Emily happiness, and always leaving Emily alone. Emily's her can't be found under the mascaraed eyes of New York's disco girls. It lies not on the soft and pampered skin of the wealthy students who study art. It is not to be discovered resting between the crevices of the vulva or along the walls of the vaginal canal. It doesn't wait anxiously in the intrauterine promise of eggs floating away their leisurely days. No dildo, no strap-on, no finger, no tongue can reach your her, Emily, because your her is what happens to magic when it coagulates into the human form: your her is a magic that needs to shit daily: your her is the ultimate dream realized in terms of the ultimate reality—the reality of the human body.

I go into my pocket, looking for my bag, but then I remember it's lying empty somewhere behind me. I settle for a cigarette. I begin to feel like I'm going to puke because the clawing inside of me is now occurring at a significantly higher frequency.

We walk for a while without saying anything; both of us are looking at the ground. I get down on my knees and brush away some snow. The lake looks like a piece of frozen glass, and I can see my reflection. It looks distorted, the same way it looks when I check myself out in the window of the subway train. I seem just as tired and just as old, and I begin to wonder if the surface of the frozen lake isn't tilted to the darkest corners of my life, like the windows of random subway trains.

"So what should I do?" Emily asks, looking toward me. I dart my eyes up to her face—the cold air freezes her tears into solid pathways across her cheeks.

"About what?"

"About her."

What should Emily do about her? How does a dreamer stop the dreaming? Where can the living go to join the rest in death? Always the easy dream shrunk down to her and him—always her, and always him.

I take a breath in through my mouth: I wish I had some coke.

"The problem with you, Em, is the way you fuck."

"What do you mean, the way I fuck?" she asks.

I get up and look at her face: her eyes are sad.

"The way you fuck, Em. You see, there are two ways to do it. You can fuck to love, or you can fuck to kill. *You* fuck to love. Every girl you're with is a partner in some kind of creation, a gateway to some sort of dream. That's beautiful and wonderful and all, but as long as you keep going at it *that* way, things are never going to change."

She doesn't say anything for a while, and I begin to think that I might have been too harsh.

"Well, what should I do differently?" she asks.

"Do what I do, Em. Make it the goal of your sex life to destroy whoever you find, and it will go away, all of it will go away. Use whatever you have to. Use switchblades, use razor blades, use fucking chain saws to cut it out of you. Hack yourself to pieces, hack away until nothing's left, until you're a fucking zero." (I begin to laugh.) "Love won't come around anymore once you've fucked yourself into a zero because zeros don't exist, they remain unlisted, and how can you locate something that's not on any map or in any guidebook?" I pause and throw my cigarette to the ground. "You can't. The best you'll get is an empty hole where once stood a dream gone mad."

I stop and get angry at myself for letting my mouth go like that. I feel really sick, and I just want a fucking line. I love Emily, but why should I get into a frenzy over her fucking problems? Why should I be honest with anyone? It's not like she's there for me when I have shit going on.

I can feel Emily staring at me, and that gets me angrier because she's probably standing there thinking that I'm an asshole; but then she says, "You're right. I have to choose. I guess I'd rather not love. I guess I'd rather not feel. I guess anything, anything's better than this."

I smile, kind of the way a benevolent hunter would smile as he stands above the carcass of some animal he just made game, happy to have ended the suffering.

We walk back to the shore and don't say anything else. When we get in the car we decide to have breakfast at the Hauppauge Palace. February's sun casts empty morning rays on the vacant parking lot. After breakfast, we go to Ray's house to pick up some coke. We come back again at night for some more. We pull into his driveway. I can see him trying to get a little girl away from the screen door, away from the soft glow of the porch light. We spend the whole night doing coke in her mother's house; and by morning, we start to get anxious, so Emily gets out her Xanax, and we each take a few to calm ourselves down.

Remember that time we did coke at your mom's house all night, Em? Remember how you just went for it, line after line after line, a meal for the mauled. Remember when the sun came up, and you just stared at me like your insides were disappearing, like you were becoming a cold and lifeless object?

I remember. I remember looking at you that night. I remember hearing the powder flow up the nostrils. I remember how the impact of crystallized dust with the lining of your nostrils reverberated through the empty house like a hollow bomb exploding, and watching you, Em, watching her, as I had never seen her before, I could tell that she was trying to kill that thing inside her, trying to kill that *her* that had followed Emily throughout her life; that *her* that had left a little girl standing in the halls of Suburban High School a secret watcher; that *her* that had kept Emily up so many nights, that had demanded so many tears and so many prayers, that the world had told Emily should have been a *him*. I see Emily as she finally kills the wish that crept into the bedroom window of her childhood house one night so long ago. I hear Emily as she snuffs the little song that grew into a terrible opera. I see Emily tear at the skin of that beloved ideal, line after line after line, like a slasher film of the soul, slash-slash-slash-slash, and I feel… guilty.

"Here you go," she says really fast, holding out a bill, crisp and epileptic. "That's for you. Those two lines. That's for you." She smiles, a crazy smile that's more like the curved line in a psychopath's drawing than anything that could be said to express something as subtle as a smile.

"Thanks."

Below me there are two perpendicular lines stretching beyond where I can see; they glisten in the light; patient blades awaiting death.

"Em, those lines... they're like fucking train tracks."

I go down.

The coke is filling me.

Piece-by-piece, the tracks are disappearing.

I do the line, and come up for air. Emily is staring at the wall; her skin glows, as an expensive lamplight hits the film of sweat covering her body.

"Are you OK?"

"Yeah. I'm OK. Do the other line."

"Give me a minute...."

The reason I felt guilty was because I didn't tell Emily the whole story about zeros. I didn't tell her how deceiving they are, about how the periphery seems harmless in its curves but how it's deadlier than the edge of scythes. I didn't give Emily the whole story because I was scared that she might choose to keep her around. I was scared that she might realize something positive about pain and suffering under the weight of ideals. I just didn't want to see my friend suffer anymore.

I knew what it felt like to really dream, to really love, and I knew how much it hurt, so I didn't tell Emily the whole story about zeros. Maybe I figured she understood the consequence of nothingness on her own.

I go back down.

The coke is filling me.

Piece by tiny piece the tracks are disappearing.

"Thanks," I say, but Emily doesn't hear; she's staring ahead at something; I look to see what's caught her in such a grip—and I see that it's the painting she had made of Lisa.

When you're falling toward the center of that empty circle, you feel like it's the only way. Then one day you wake up and find yourself alive under a frozen sheet of ice. You claw, and you claw, and you claw away, day-after-day-after-day-after-day, until that morning comes and shines its light on a pair of tired hands that have finally stopped the clawing, a pair of beautiful hands that have succeeded in their mission and move no more. What else are you supposed to do, though? When you're filled with passion and love and wonder, when all you can do is dream and desire in a world that's being crushed under the weight of freezing things, it feels like living your life in the coldest part of Hell anyway; so, who cares? This Hell's so frozen that the word *is* disappears from language because *is* requires movement and in this Hell there *is no movement—there is simply stasis and an accompanying rot.* So, why care?

It's a slow torture, an unseen torture, to be so moved among all the plastic images of my time. To be young these days is to be one in a million, a one so rare that mostly everyone else seems like swathes of dawnlit wheat in wasted fields. Most people can't see the soul anymore because most people today are old and dead. They've become so much like the things they worship that slowly they themselves are becoming things. And as things, people only assume you're in pain if you have a bloody nose or a bruise—if the mechanics of your physicality seem out of whack. But the pain of the body is nothing when juxtaposed to the suffering suffocation of the soul—and all unseen, all unacknowledged suffering gains the full force of torture. I felt guilty, but I shouldn't have. It's so cold in this Hell that the only way to tolerate it is to numb a little bit here and a little bit there. The only way out is to pretend, each to each, in our own way, so that we might feast with the pretenders for one more day.

I ask Emily if everything's OK. She says nothing. She just keeps staring at that painting of Lisa, staring at the gentle motions of paint she had once danced out of her deepest self, staring, and becoming an unfeeling statue, as if to counteract the testament of that her, which she, my friend Emily, once had been.

I'm walking down the BOWERY with Tara. We're walking from work to Marion's, where Josh is DJing. I've decided not to do any coke tonight, and as a universal jest it's just started to snow along the BOWERY. The whole world of night takes on a new dimension of lonely steel and concrete, peopled with the lost, smoking in a snowstorm.

Marion's is almost empty. I'm not surprised. Marion's is a mixed-up place. There's no scene that goes on there, and most of the time it's just an addendum to the Slide, which is underground, its cavernous entrance next door. You'll mostly find yuppies *sitting* at the bar in Marion's. *Standing* at the bar you get a different perspective, discovering the fags from downstairs, who got tired of waiting for a drink at the Slide or who are waiting for a friend to use Marion's bathroom because their friend got tired of waiting to use the bathroom at the Slide, or who just used the bathroom at Marion's themselves and now need a drink, quickly! Around the DJ booth you'll find those same kids of New York you see everywhere you go, slowly expanding into the emptying tables of Marion's restaurant section.

We say hi to Josh, then take the table right underneath the low DJ booth. I put my bag on the floor; and Tara, after some hesitation and uncertainty, agrees to let Josh hold her bag behind the booth. I smile at how much Josh's hustler reputation has caught up with him. It feels nice when your friends fail.

"What are you smiling at?" he asks.

"Nothing. Absolutely nothing."

Taking the stem of the Cosmo glass, I begin to feel that stirring in my center. I want a line, and there's really no reason—I just do. Seeing Josh always makes me want a line; but a lot of things make me want a line. It's worse when I can actually smell the coke like I can when I'm near Josh. Tara's also smiling now as we lower to the table synchronistically with our drinks, laughing about something, and my head gets foggy and then light as the first mouthfuls of the Cosmo hit the walls of my mouth. A fog invades Marion's, and for a minute I'm all alone, listening to Electroclash beats, seeing Cheshire smiles reveal rotting teeth, everything sounding and looking like cocaine. I keep talking to Tara, pretending that everything is fine, and then I look up and see Greg: tall, beautiful Greg. The fog fades. I jump up to hug you; I feel the long absent familiarity of your hands on my mid-back and the hazy parameters of your hips against my belly and the heat that always rose from you, like there was a furnace underneath that gorgeous flesh. The fog disappears, leaving the air more chilled than before. My arms around Greg, I give in; I'll make that phone call tonight.

"Sit down, Greg, sit down. Do you know Tara?"

They shake hands. They are saying hello.

"What's going on?" I say, resting my hand on his knee.

He smiles and looks straight into me.

"Nothing, you know. Things are good. Things are really good actually."

I put my glass down. I look at him, look at his chest, his thighs. I remember his feet.

Greg met me three years ago at the Cock. I was dancing on the stage with some kids. There I am—three years younger, still downtown. I'm wearing a Confederate hat I bought at the Costume shop on Broadway, and John-John's playing some music we're all in love with, "destroy everything you touch," and the place is full, "destroy me this way," and the backroom's open, "anything that may desert you, so it cannot hurt you," to repair the frayed fabric of boy love— "everything-you-touch, you-don't-feel, do-not-know, what-you-steal, destroy everything you touch, to-day, (please) destroy me this way...." I look down—I see Josh talking up some people by the stage, and occasionally they look up at me—I can see that Josh really loves me by the way his face shows so much pride at how crazy I am, and then I see this tall, beautiful boy, this new and fresh boy, this boy who would become Greg. The colors seemed to stop moving on everyone except you. All I could make sense of was this boy who looked like he just walked out of my past or the past I wished I had had. But that was only for a second. I looked away, gathered myself, and rejoined reality.

Greg's the one who came up to me, right up to the stage, and asked me my name. I stepped down to hear him better, and fifteen minutes later we were making out in his car. I felt his dick; it was already bloated. He did some coke from his house key. I rubbed his cock through the barrier of used denim fabric. My insides were exploding with pre-cum, pre-cum from the stomach, pre-cum from the brain, and the duodenum is twisting the juices through the tunnel of myself making my ass wet. Greg asks, "Do you want to get a motel room?"

And I fall in love. "Yeah, sure. Where do you want to go?" "We can go anywhere," he says, getting his car in motion. "Let's go to Jersey." He laughs beautifully, and we're heading across the GW Bridge, and I'm falling in love, that special kind of love, that cocaine kind of love. "I can't wait to suck your cock," I say. He looks over and smiles. His eyes travel down my body, and his smile grows in proportion to the distance covered by his eyes.

He turns on the radio and I hear *"If you're going to San.—Fran.—Cisco,"* and the night is speckled by the terrestrial stars of the city lights, and I'm so happy, so fucking happy right at this moment, high and happy and high.

Before that night, I hadn't left New York since I had returned from college. I forgot what it was like to ride around in a car at night on unknown highways, but to ride around with a boy looking for a motel room where we'd fuck all night with bags of cocaine as fuel in my right pocket, that was something I had never known.

Greg told me a little about himself that night. He was "from Vermont" (could have guessed that from the license plate) and his sister was "in the circus" (not that). No one really knew that Greg was gay. That's why we weren't going back to his place. For money, he drove "one of those bikes that carry tourists around in carriages."

"Really?" I say, laughing.

"Why are you laughing?" he asks, looking over.

"I just hadn't heard that one before." Every word he speaks, every move he makes, fades the rest of the world away. "Usually it's like I'm a waiter or I'm a bartender or I throw parties, but that one—that one's new."

I unzip his jeans and wiggle the head of his cock out. His face is filled with pleasure as I begin to rub the thick and growing head around.

"You're trouble. I can't wait to get at you tonight," he says looking over; his eyes are sweet; he is just a horny boy who happens to be beautiful.

"How 'bout you?"

"How 'bout me what?"

"What do *you* do?"

"I write."

"For money?"

Pause.

"I wait tables."

I let go of his cock.

"Greg, why does no one know you're gay?"

His smile fades.

"It's not that no one knows."

His smile fades.

He gently zips his pants, adding, "I love that a lot, but I have to drive."

His smile disappears.

I light up a cigarette. If I can't have the cock, I'll settle for the truth.

"Your roommates don't know."

"I'm not ashamed or anything, if that's what you think. Some people know, it's just—I'm not a big fan of the whole gay culture thing in New York, it seems so fake. I want to be more than a party boy or a fashionista."

"That makes sense. Gay New York's a TV sitcom."

I pause looking out the window into the low-lying civilizations of New Jersey.

"Would you ever even have a boyfriend?"

"Oh yeah." Greg says. "Of course. I would come out for him and everything, but it would have to be the right guy. I'm waiting for the right guy."

Dylan comes on; I decide to let it go.

"This mix is great. Your taste in music's awesome, Greg."

"Really, aren't you like an eighties boy?" he says putting his hand on my belly. He smiles beautifully.

"I love Dylan. That was such a cool fucking time, man. We sure missed out," he says getting his hand underneath my shirt.

> *Through this open world*
> *I'm a-bound to ramble,*
> *through ice and snow,*
> *sleet and rain.*

"We sure did."

> *I'm a-bound to ride that morning railroad,*
> *perhaps I'll die upon that train.*

"So, what's so good about things, Gregie. Don't keep us in the dark."

"Well, you'll like this one—I have a boyfriend."

Oh.

Say something....

Say something, like you don't care.

"That's great, a boyfriend." I take a large sip from my Cosmo glass. "A boy who's more than a friend.... Where is he?"

Greg looks around. "He's here, somewhere."

"He's here?" I ask, frightened. I put the elliptical edge of my martini glass to my lips and take a big gulp.

"Yeah, you might know him. Josh knows him. His name is Jeremy. Oh—there he is."

Greg raises his hand to call over a boy. A boy walks over. He's more beautiful than Greg, more beautiful than me. He's a tall boy with pale skin and curly black hair that's grown out, and blue eyes, and long legs, and a toned body below his tight jeans and t-shirt.

"This is my boyfriend—Jeremy."

When it's my turn to shake Jeremy's hand, I look into his eyes: in them I see my now lost past with Greg.

We walk into the motel room. The first thing I do is *kiss* Greg. My cock is really hard. Greg's cock is really hard. I make two lines stretching halfway across the table between the two queen-size beds. I do mine. Greg has his shirt off, and I hand him the dollar bill. While he's doing his line I get into my underwear leaving my tube socks pulled high to my knees. He rises to where I'm standing and observes me for a moment. He observes me with his hands, with his fingers; then he starts to observe me with his mouth, kissing me on the neck, on the nipples. He raises my right hand high and licks my armpit, and then he looks at me and pulls his lips slowly into mine. When a boy is kissing you on the mouth, he is kissing you and nothing less than you. When a boy puts his lips on yours, he wants the very air you breathe. A boy who goes for the mouth is a boy who can't simply settle for the cock or the ass. A boy who goes for the mouth is hungry for essence.

I'm on my knees against the wall. We're both naked. Greg's fucking my mouth, and I look up at him. His facial muscles are taut with concentration and pulled across the skull by exertion and power and strength. I feel the head of his cock plug my throat, and I can't breathe. Coke in the nose and cock in the mouth, and I can't breathe. He leaves it there for a moment, the swollen head resting on the back of my throat, and strokes his hand along my cheeks.

"God, that's fucking beautiful," he says looking down at me.

My mouth's clamping down on his cock. I remain still, in a strange drug meditation on the power of love.

We keep doing coke all night. We're covered with baby oil. Greg does a line off my ass. Then he goes to eat what he left behind. Then he spreads my cheeks and puts the whole force of his tongue on my hole. I let out a groan. He begins to rub his cock up and down along my lubed back, and I ask him to fuck me. He says, "Yeah you want to get fucked boy?" I groan. I'm on top of him, and he's guiding me down down down onto him. I look into his eyes, but I can't understand a thing about them because eyes are filled with beauty and I'm not really capable of understanding beauty at the present moment. It's like those receptors have been anaesthetized, or paralyzed, or lobotomized. I feel him, the big hands on my hips guiding me down, and the cock in my ass raising me up, as I vacantly stare into those two meaningless globes tensed in the crevices of his head.

G reg and I got together again a couple of times over the next year. I'd usually be the one to call, and then we'd meet in a bar and have a drink while we waited for my dealer to arrive. Once we got the coke we'd drive to a motel room out in New Jersey and fuck all night. Except the last time. The last time we met, we drove up the Taconic to a place somewhere near Poughkeepsie. He would have kept driving, but I finally told him to stop. I wanted him so fucking bad, and the desire and all the coke we were doing on the drive up north began to fry my nerves so that I began to see the flashing sirens of my warped imagination nearing possibility.

After all my morning-afters with Greg, I would get this notion that I had to leave New York. For some reason, I felt alive when I was out of that city; and the things I did with Greg felt like an attempt at resurrecting love. It wasn't like when I met boys in New York and spent the whole night rolling around naked with them, fucking in cabs and strange bedrooms, which were all actually the same room placed in different locales of time and place. I look at all those boys now, all those bodies failing to combine, happening at once, as they fall haphazardly into my memory to create a scene of final orgy. I see these bodies, mine and theirs; and I see that

51

these bodies enswathed in the sheets of various unknowns are but exequies for love.

On the drive home that morning from some motel room south of Poughkeepsie, I felt it most strongly, that premonition to leave. I looked out at the hills and felt the summer air and knew that I had to go. But I never did. I just couldn't abandon the hope that New York might turn around; that it still had a future; that it still had a chance.

Greg told me he was going to sell his car soon. He was upset because his mom called in the middle of our fucking and told him she was sick. I didn't care, not about the warnings from the air, or that he was going to sell his car, or that his mom was sick. I was sitting in the passenger seat poisoned and trying not to die. I looked into the sky and wished that I could somehow disappear so that I wouldn't have to deal with any of this anymore.

I still hear him saying it that first night, still remember what he looked like when he said it. "We can go anywhere." There's a time in life that you can go anywhere. Car or no car. Greg or no Greg. And if you don't, you'll begin to die, and others will begin to die around you, and your life will become a game of who can eat away faster—at themselves and at their friends. You'll get tired, and the world will become too small. That's what it means to get old—the boundaries of the world expand and take over the frontiers, and somehow everything seems smaller and deader because it's all been done and it's all been seen. Somehow the wonder disappears; and without wonder, the world becomes as boring as a life unlived stalking a Sunday morning.

Jeremy's eyes have long disappeared from mine, leaving me mesmerized by what I had. Watching Greg and Jeremy pat each other gently across the territory of their bodies, I sense how much older I've become, how much colder, how much more dead. I begin to wonder if this communication between these two beautiful boys is what love is all about. I forgot how gentle love is when it materializes into the form of bodies touching kindly, and I begin to think that what I had with Greg was not really an attempt at resurrecting love. What Greg and I had was not a gentle wandering; it was not an attempt at two separated beings trying to unite in tactile communication. What Greg and I had was violent and angry. It wasn't anything like love. If it was anything, what Greg and I had, it was just a materialization of hate. I was still trying to kill you, and Greg was still trying to kill the possibility that he might be gay. And we were trying to do that, as the boys who love to kill will do, by killing each other with the brutality of the cock and the vigilante movements of our anxious cumshot. We could have strangled one another on those motel nights, which are doomed to forever rest in their untouchable distances outside New York, if we had simply known how much we actually hated each other and ourselves.

Josh gets done DJing and tells us that he has to go to the Westside to work an after-hours. I call my dealer and tell him to meet us at the spot. Outside, the snowfall has overtaken the world. Lost children chase each other along the abandoned streets. Tara decides not to come because she has to work in the morning. We hail a cab for her; and it slowly moves off toward Williamsburg. We get one for ourselves, and the four of us—me, Josh, Jeremy and Greg—get in and head to some new after-hours somewhere on the Westside.

I spend a lot of time sitting across from Greg while Jeremy dances around the empty place. There are a couple of girls around and some guys by the bar, and everyone looks like they're waiting for something. I look across the empty dance floor, which has a thin layer of carpet on the ground, and see that there's another room in the back. Through the open doorway I can tell that some kind of card game's going on, and I can see money flying around and cigarette smoke trying to escape and some faceless guys who never move their eyes away from the table.

"Are you surprised?" Greg asks me.

"Am I what?"

"Surprised, you know—about Jeremy."

He looks at me with his brown eyes: in them I find no narrative of our lost past.

"Well, a little—yeah."

"He's beautiful isn't he? We're really in love."

"I'm happy for you Greg," I tell him; and I *am* happy for him.

Greg's so normal, so fortunately normal. What would it have been like to have been that normal, to have been like everyone else, to have grown up in Vermont or Massachusetts and not know anything but the comfort of late night car drives and front yard trees? What would it have been like to have a room I could run to and a concrete history of comfort that was always there? How would it have felt if everything wasn't so shattered, and if I couldn't feel how shattered everything was? I bet it would have been nice.

There's a clinking sound as Greg mixes the ice around in his vodka tonic.

"You know it's not that I didn't want a boyfriend. I always wanted to have a boyfriend, it's just that it had to be the right guy. Take me and you for example. That was a lot of fun, man, but it's not like it would have ever gone beyond what it was."

The whole time he's saying it, he's looking at Jeremy. I search for spite in his voice, but I fail to find it. He turns to me—and adds, "You know, you're just not that type of guy." I smile, recalling the confident ignorance love provides. "You know me, Greg: sex, drugs, and suicide." He laughs (uncomfortably?), bringing me into existence for the first time tonight. I look at him and feel horrible.

Jeremy's in the bathroom with me doing a bump. He says, "I want to kiss you." He's leaning against the tiled wall, and I'm looking across the tiny parameters of the white stall into his eyes, searching for some more of my lost history with Greg. I find nothing, and I give up.

His knee is bent, and it reaches toward me, so I grab it and slowly move my hand up to his thigh. I can feel the muscle pressing against the fabric of his faded jeans. "Then let's kiss," I say. He looks at me and says, no, he can't, it's too early with Greg. "I really love Greg, but you're so beautiful." He does another bump. I tell him we should leave.

He agrees.

On the way out, I suggest a threesome. Jeremy likes my suggestion; but after he asks Greg, he comes back to tell me that Greg said no. The rest of the night Greg avoids me, and Jeremy keeps looking over at me with these eyes that can't control themselves from the invisible pull of my direction. I invite his stare, hoping to fully destroy everything I had with Greg. I find it an easy thing to do.

Nothing really hurt me during those days because I lived in a fantasy. As long as you're high, life's a permanent vacation. It's not a pleasant vacation or a terrible vacation—it's just a vacation. As long as you're high, you vacate the boring and pressing matters of the everyday world. But one day, the vacation ends; and you come back to find that while you were away the world kept moving, that time kept passing, and everything you used to have rotted away simply because you weren't there to take care of it—simply because you were *on vacation*. That had yet to happen; but already, I feel the rust of neglect descending on my numb, uncaring bones.

The place is closing, and Josh tells me about an after-after-hours we're going to. I tell Jeremy and Greg that they should come, but Greg doesn't want to. Outside, the sun has risen; but the sky is pillowed with a thick sheet of clouds. The snow's stopped falling, but the cement ground of the early New York morning is covered in snow, which piles a couple of feet into the air. The streets are bathed in that surreal grey, which comes about from mixing sleepless nights, cocaine, and a heavy snowfall that has just passed a concrete world.

"Come on, let's go," Josh tells me.

"Where are we going?"

"To some girl's—where is she?—to her house," Josh says, pointing to a short girl who looks like she's been here all her life. I ask Greg and Jeremy once more if they're sure they don't want to come.

"Come on Greg, I'd like to go. It would be fun," Jeremy says.

"No, I don't want to. I'm really tired."

"Girl, let's go." Josh says, getting annoyed. Greg and Jeremy say good-bye. I stare at them as they walk away. I see the backs of two boys who are being pulled westward to the Hudson River. I see two boys in the snow gently pushing each other, two children who have finally found a home, and their home is the proximity of one to the other, the prelude of distinct bodies journeying to a private place where they will meet and become complete. No one exists at that moment but a fragmented pair, soon to be made whole: a one made whole by two.

"I know what you were doing there, girl," Josh tells me in the cab.

Muffled through the radio, I hear Robert Palmer advising me to admit it, my addiction to love.

"You're so stupid," Josh says with a laugh. "I just don't get you."

Some kid's doing a bump on the other side of Josh, and the girl who's taking us to the after-after-hours is in the front, staring into the rearview mirror. Josh tells the kid to give him a bump, and I want to ask for one too, but I can't move: I'm paralyzed in some familiar trap. On the corner, a lady's standing with her dog, who's turning the white snow into a piss slushie. No one else is on the street, and I'm torn between physical pain and emotional joy, and emotional pain and physical joy.

The after-after-hours is in someone's basement apartment. There are no windows, and a big black stage extends into the center of the main room. I'm talking to some graffiti artists, and they say we should get together and write. I ask them if they've ever been down to the N-line's graffiti row. No, never. I ask them how long they've been writing, and they tell me they've been writing since the mid-nineties, ever since they were in junior high, and that they mostly write in the Bronx, where both of them are from. The girl who brought us to the party asks if I want to promote some party she's doing at some club I've never heard of. I say sure, knowing that this is all just bullshit high on a lot of coke.

The room is filled with kids, but no one's here. There are no windows, and there is no such thing as time. Someone asks if I need anything, and I go with him to the bathroom and buy two bags. I tell him I'll be right out, and he leaves the bathroom. I go to the mirror and see something that looks like me. Someone's knocking on the door, and I don't do any of the coke. I just stand there and watch that thing in the mirror, that crazy looking thing, and wonder where I've gone. I try to find myself, but I can't. It's like I've disappeared and left this strange thing behind as my suicide letter. No words, no paper folded neatly into an envelope, just a scared boy that's falling. I am falling, I am falling, somewhere in my life the snow is falling with me to the ground.

R, R, R, R, R, Vandalism is a crime, Reward up to $500 for the arrest and conviction of anyone who commits Graffiti, Call 911 to report crimes in progress, darkdarkdark, ligggght ligggght, 311 to provide information, *Mr. Kazmierczak grew up on a tree-lined street of ranch-style homes in the suburbs of Chicago. "He was an exemplary student and a nice guy," said Kristen Myers, one of his professors. "Something dreadful must have happened to him."* Do not lean on door, lightdarklight, Do not hold doors, dark, 36 Street,…

The drive to the train station began in silence.

A hard rain had begun to fall, smashing against the moving car. Its drops infringed on the human silence with whispers of violence. The windshield wipers would reveal brief moments of green silhouettes colored by the soft shades of a pleasant evening.

"Nancy, remember when you used to wake us up for our beach days at Smith Point?"

The car accelerated. Her determined eyes watched the road.

"One night before one of those trips, I told Emily something."

The car increased in speed. I looked at the odometer: 80, 85, 90.

"Did she ever talk about that night?"

The car slowed: 95, 89, 70.

"What are you talking about?" she asked in a low voice.

"One night before we went to Smith Point."

"Who, who went to Smith Point?"

Her voice rose.

The odometer steadied: 65, 60.

"Me. And Emily."

"Shut up! Shut up! SHUT UP!" she yelled. The car swerved. The rain continued its assault upon any attempts at silence.

The car—a 2008 Infiniti FX45—idled at an angle, blocking both lanes on the private road. From the corner of my eyes, I could see Nancy, her hands gripping the steering wheel, her blank face staring ahead.

We didn't move until two headlights beamed into the car, followed by the loud and angry sound of a car horn.

The car stopped right by the train tracks. I was too numb to say anything to her, so I just put my hand on the door and pushed it open. I could hear the thunder in the eastern distance. Then I heard her voice.

"Smith Point," she said. "You used to go there together in the summer."

I looked at her. She was looking ahead.

"Yes, we did."

The thundering rain continued its violent attack on the world.

"It feels like America's become a nightmare."

She paused. Then,

"I never want to see you again."

"You won't."

After the train started moving, I locked myself in the bathroom. I took out a bag and did bumps from it intermittently. The train went *Choo-choo, Choo-choo—Sweeeee!* I tried to cry, but I couldn't; and eventually I had to return to my seat.

I got out at Penn Station, and I didn't know where to go. The thought of going uptown and seeing Jack, or running away to Coney Island made me sick. I couldn't answer any questions, but I couldn't be alone. I needed to go somewhere that was home, be around people that could substitute family and insinuate place, so I got on the pay phone and called David to see if he wanted to go to the Cock.

His voice crackles over the line, "Sure, meet me at my place in Williamsburg."

Do not lean on door; Do not hold doors; IF YOU SEE SOMETHING, SAY SOMETHING; THE NEW YORK TIMES, I see graffiti scattered, I see ads everywhere, I see a newspaper, NATIONAL, I see a train filled with blank faces and strained mouths, SATURDAY, but I say nothing, FEBRUARY 16, I see a face that's too young to be this tired, 2008, but I say nothing, *DeKALB, Ill.—The day after five students were gunned down in an afternoon science class on the campus of Northern Illinois University here, survivors struggled to manage their grief as the authorities released more details about the shooting and the gunman.* Pacific Street, Atlantic Avenue, Pacific Street, Atlantic Avenue,...

The sun had long set by the time I got to David's. I was hoping to see the birds make their circles around the buildings of Williamsburg, but I was too late.

As David cut some lines, I noticed a typed piece I had written for him scotch-taped at its corners to a wall that was drowned out by baby pictures, ticket stubs from shows dating as far back as the '94 LOLLAPALOOZA concert at RANDALL'S ISLAND, and glossy cutouts of young boys staring out into nothing while jerking off. *The slaughter of the innocents is the slaughter of ideals and passions. The slaughter of the innocents is the numbing of the soul. The slaughter of the innocents is the final death of dreams. Youthanasia.*

I still had a lot of bags from the stay on Long Island, but we decided it was best to get some more, so we did, and then we did a couple of bags, and then everything was better. We took the L train into the city, and I kept putting my sunglasses on, then taking them off, paranoid about all the people around us. We got out at 6 Avenue and walked what seemed a mile to the F train platform. Some old guy was singing, strumming his guitar, stomping on the ground with his right foot—"*And I'm gettin' old.... And I'm gettin' old....*"

The train took forever getting to the station. David and I just sat on the bench, expectation and anxiety rising. "*Keep me searching for a heart of gold.*" The guy kept singing, and David finally said, "God I wish he'd shut the fuck up. Someone should shoot all these fucking bums." And then the train pulled in—its surface empty dull silver, revealing a serpent that has lost its skin and cannot reproduce a new one.

The Cock was disappointing; but we stayed until the end, and before I left I bought some more coke. David told me that he finished "*Less Than Zero,*" and in the bathroom, between lines, he wondered out loud what it would be like to overdose for good. I didn't respond because I was thinking about that boy I had seen outside; but now I wonder what it would be like, not only to overdose but to die. Would it be anything like what's happening to the scarred horizon? Is death full of so much blackness mixing with so much rare color, like it's trying to get at the full spectrum of things all in one moment? I remember looking around me and I felt so tired, like I had lived forever; and now I wondered if the Cock was really boring, or if it was just me, or if it was a mixture of the two.

"So, what do you think it would be like?" David asks, taking a large bump off his key. "You know, having a serious overdose? Do you think you'd die?"

He stops, leaving a key plowed into the emptying bag of coke, then says, "Do you think it'd be better than *this*?"

And I wondered looking around at the boys searching, and the coke addicts snorting, and all the people promoting themselves, and all the people sitting in the corner and watching, and David's bag, which was so full a minute before and now was so empty, would it, would death be better than this? I kept thinking about that boy I had seen outside, that beautiful young boy with black hair, and I wondered where he went. He was a perfect boy, and he smelled like dreams; and like all perfect boys, he abandoned, leaving only his image and his breath to feed on.

The world is silent when heard through a Coney Island dawn. Here, at this time, all I can hear is that ghost. All I can hear is that dying city as she gasps for air at the ocean's edge. Here is where she comes between the dying of night and the breaking of day. Here is where she comes, New York, comes like a broken window seeking to mend interstitial space, comes lonely to a still and familiar place, comes nostalgic for her former self, and holds vigil on the morning shores of Coney Island. Here, at the time of night's death approaching, New York comes to remember what it was like to be alive.

I look across the amusement park. The roller coaster curves upward like a twisted spine. The Ferris wheel hugs the winds for comfort. The sun rises into the dark waters. I am crashing to the ground. The train arrives, and I get on, Manhattan bound. I reach into my bag, and it's filled with bags of coke—untouched bags, empty bags, half full bags. I must have twenty bags of coke on me right now. I look around. No one's on the train, so I take one of the full bags, roll a dollar bill, empty it. I reach into my bag to get more coke; a blue envelope falls to the floor. Staring at it, I begin to wonder what I'm doing and where I'm going.

I remember recently running into this girl who used to go to school with us on the bus heading into Bushwick. She mentioned you. She said you were living upstate in Red Hook. I thought of the letter in that blue envelope lying on the floor. I couldn't believe its words were true. *I had to make sure that its words were not true.* I decided then that I had to see you. I decided then to take the train to Poughkeepsie. To Poughkeepsie. From New York. Broken cities, broken hearts, broken dreams.

I picked the letter up from the floor and placed it gently back into my bag.

I would see if she was right. I knew that Poughkeepsie would prove her wrong.

The doors close. The train begins its journey north.

Mr. Kazmierczak carried out his attack in a matter of seconds, the authorities said, even with stopping to reload his shotgun, ultimately shooting 16 students and the teacher, all between the ages of 18 and 32. The authorities on Friday identified the dead as Daniel Parmenter, 20; Catalina Garcia, 20; Ryanne Mace, 19; Julianna Gehant, 32; and Gayle Dubowski, 20. All were from Illinois.

The porn's called "All American Gang Bang." Except for the naked body that's splayed out on a center table, everyone else is wearing symbols signifying America—one kid has a flag draped around his shoulders; another kid has a football helmet resting on his head; a third kid is wearing military boots, and once in a while he moves a whip through the air landing it on the back of the naked boy's body. The shots keep changing, and the TV breathes like an asthmatic through the edited material; but that boy keeps getting fucked, his hands tied behind his back, his feet tied to the edge of the table, his cheeks being slapped by the strong hands of a tall, beautiful boy who teases him and makes him beg for a long, hard dick. Occasionally, there's that whip across the back. The boy can't do anything but muffle out noise because his head is being jammed into the long cock of the tall, beautiful boy.

Josh is by my side. In between the scenes I tell him that Emily called and that I'm going out to Long Island. He says, "Cool," uncaringly, mesmerized by the epileptic story on the screen.

I look at the porn and see that same boy being fucked in that same way, this time by two different guys. I look away, trying to catch something that will help me escape, but nothing comes, so my eyes begin to tear small cold tears. I catch the reflection of two bodies in one of the mirrors surrounding the bed. They're bathed in the changing tones of a violent light. The room has faded into violet shadows.

Josh puts out his cigarette and hands me the CD case on which the coke bag and the razor blade lay crossed. I try to open the bag, but my hands are covered in lube, so I just tear it at the top. I put the straw into the bag and take a big inhale, careful to leave enough for one extra jolt later on. When I pull the straw out of my nose, some of the coke begins to fall out of the nostril—like a brief snowfall, so I tilt my head back and do a couple of deep, hard snorts, hoping the earthquake can clear up my clogged sinuses. It works, and I get a big rush throughout my body, like I've been electrocuted.

The TV keeps moaning and groaning. I look at the screen—and there I am, getting fucked by a long train of bodies whose heads are cut off at the top of the screen. Boy after boy after boy comes to take his turn. I begin to recognize the bodies. There's Logan's pierced left nipple, and Chris's stomach, which once got exposed at the Hole and drove me nuts—all I needed was "for you to fuck me." There, Lars's feet, and there, that boy from New Jersey who was a carpenter and who fucked me in the Howard Johnson on E HOUSTON ST, his chest straining, his hands pushing. There's River's reflection in the mirror, as I'm lying on his floor duct-taped-at-my-hands-and-knees: he's staring at my ass; it quivers under the recent beatings of his belt. I see boys whose names I can't remember, and familiar bodies of I'm-here-for-one-night-only strangers. They keep coming, one after the other, and I begin to wonder if I'll see you, but the train just keeps coming, the boys just keep coming, one after the other, a-thunder-and-a-clash, and I realize that you won't be among the crowd.

I see the eyes of the boy who's getting fucked on the screen: they're hungry for love, desperate for perfection, and they keep wondering, as the headless boys roll through, one after the other, if this one's it, if this is the guy who's actually Prince Charming, hiding underneath the sexual brutality. His eyes flicker against the expectation—flit from one onto the other—fly from him to only flutter within the fleshy wind; and they keep coming, faster and faster, more and more, faster and faster, more more, faster, faster, more-more-more—and I begin to wonder if this train is ever going to end, and then I look out the window and it's snowing, it's snowing, all of a sudden there's nothing but the snow. And I remember that somewhere in my life the snow is falling.

When I wake up, I look over—I see Josh. He's sitting on the edge of the bed eating a bowl of cereal and watching TV. There are rockets and tanks fighting somewhere in the Middle East. He looks over at me and smiles.

"Good morning," he says. "You hungry?"

"Have you slept?" I ask.

"No, I went out after you crashed."

"Where?"

"Doesn't matter. Did you sleep with River?"

I see Josh. I see tears in the eyes of Josh.

"Yeah, but who cares?"

"I care," he says pointing his sad eyes at me, "because you're my friend."

I take out a bag, cut a large line, and do it.

"Look Josh, you and River are long over. Just—let it go."

"You're a fucking asshole! You make me feel trapped and useless just like everyone else! River's all I had! You should know better than anyone how this *feels*!"

I don't say anything, because I don't care; I *can't* care anymore.

"It never changes," he says, looking down. "It never fucking changes."

As I'm doing a line to deal with Josh's drama, he tells me that he loves me. I stop for a second, the frayed precipice of the bill scraping my right nostril. I can't seem to understand him. Love? I recognize the word, but only as a shapeless sound. I can comprehend a subject trying to convey some notion to an object through a four-lettered verb. I can sense that I'm the object, and I can sense that Josh is the subject. I can tell he's in the beginning and I'm at the end. It's just that connecting word, that expression of action or sensation that confuses me. It's those four letters, that tight bridge where vowel follows consonant once and then again. It's that creation of a-hard-obstructed-noise-preceding-the-unobstructed-articulation-of-signal-and-staring-into-a-broken-mirror-(broken window broken glass SMITH 9TH ST.)-to-reveal-a-distorted-vision-of-one-combined-self where I get lost. I try to find out where I've heard that noise before, that noise of l-o-v-e, but instead of opening up, the four letters just collapse into each other. I try to find out what it means, search for it desperately, and I finally find a tiny thing cowering in a cold corner. I look at it, and it spells out hate. It calls me forward. I bend down to hear what it has to say. It tells me that I've found what I've been searching for: I've found what's happened to my love. It's been shriveled by every lie, by every neglect, by every disappointment in my life, and it, that thing once called love, begs me to help it die.

"I love you so much, but you have to go. I don't want to numb myself with friends anymore. Friends don't exist. I'm really all alone." I see Josh. I turn to look in the mirror—and he's not there. In the flickering violet, I do two more lines; I get dressed; I leave. Walking to the train station, a part of me wished that I still cared, but I don't. I'm not capable of caring anymore. I'm not capable of anything except falling. I am falling, I am falling, like a heavy snow. Somewhere in my life I'm falling—

And that somewhere is now.

There's a faltering in motion.

The sun's rays cross the water, landing on my face: it feels like neon light. The sun's rays are flickering epileptically, unsure, through the window. B-b-b-black. Li-li-li-light. I see my eyes: they have become two black uneven globes: eclipses with blue corona. I go into my bag and feel around for my sunglasses; I find my sunglasses; I put my sunglasses on the bridge of my nose, and then fasten them behind my ears. "Ladies and gentlemen, we have traffic up ahead on the bridge. We apoLOGIZE FOR THE WAIT AND THANK YOU FOR YOUR PATIENCE." D, D, D, a roar and Dis-Dis-Dis-Dis, blaccck-k-k-k-k-k—light: MANfred, MUTZ, (I am moving but I have no control over the motion.), SMiRK, KaZ, Hy, JESUS SAVES, Hy, LeS, liggg, Brooklyn Br, hhht, Ba, Ba, Ba, green windowpanes, No Clearance, buildings, DUMBO, WATCHTOWER, 8:46, 24°, 8:46, -4c, and the old stone bridge across from me hovering in the air.

Below the bridge, the East River palpitates like the membrane of something struggling for breath, like a thing wholly squirming from an unseen pain that's so old, time and distance can't measure it. I see waves of dark water pulsating in a meager light, heavy with recall: they are rolling away, numb to the morning, numb to the night. The sun's light quivers along the lenses of my sunglasses, then dives from the bridge to catch a small wave and give it a white outline. The wave bends to cast the outline off, and in so doing, shoots the light up to its crest in an asterisk formation: and for one moment the light beam becomes a star. And the East River is an unwilling galaxy of momentary asterisks; a galaxy that mesmerizes me with its silent beats of flashing asterisks across languid waves until, suddenly, all the music of New York's departed nights hits me like a dirge. Bauhaus at the Bank: *The bats have left the bell tower, the victims have been bled, red velvet lines, the black box, Bela Lugosi's dead.* Kim Gordon at the Pyramid: *There's something shifting in the distance, don't know what it is, day's as dead as night, except for the feeling that's crawling-up-inside-of-me, as you sing your song.* The Velvet Underground at the Factory: *I am tired, I am weary, I could sleep for a thousand years, a thousand dreams that would awake me*—all lost, swept away for commercial malls, high rents, a land with no cause, no breaks, nowhere to go in body and in mind, 8:46, MECK, CHuPA, LeS, SeNA, LeS, LeS, SeNA, MOSK, MECK, MOSK, MUTZ, the Dom, the Mudd Club, Coney Island High, Area, Save the Robots, 9:03, refuse of past youth gone, flowing in the tired river, the beat of this requiem pulsating through the sunlight beams and the wavelight sparkles into my eyes.

I go back and see forgotten images, hear forgotten words. Through a child's eyes, I watch the television screen of the nineteen-eighties: *Four years ago, I spoke to you of a new beginning and we have accomplished that. It's a good time for the great taste—Thunder-Thunder-Thunder-Thundercats—of McDonalds. We believed then and now there are no limits to growth and human progress when men and women are free to follow their dreams. The biggest taste you've ever found. Coke is it! The one that never lets you down. Coke is it! The most refreshing taste around—Coke-is-it! These will be years when our values of faith, family, work, and neighborhood were restated for a modern age; when America (crackle, crackle) turned the tide of history away from totalitarian darkness and into the warm sunlight of human freedom.*

(APPLAUSE! APPLAUSE! TEN-SECONDS-OF-APPLAUSE!)

"My friends (*crackle, crackle*) we live in a world that is lit by lightning (*crackle, crackle, crackle*) a settler pushes west and sings a song, and the song echoes out forever and fills the unknowing air (*crackle*) It is the American sound (*crackle, crackle*) That's our heritage (*crackle*) that's our song (*crackle, crackle*) We sing it still (*crackle, crackle, crackle*) God bless you (*crackle*) and may God bless America."

(APPLAUSE! APPLAUSE! MORE-THAN-TEN-SECONDS-OF-APPLAUSE!)

I'm halfway across the bridge. I feel tears fill my eyes and bubble up secretly underneath my sunglasses. For my generation, born in those great eighties, to come of age in these double zeros, television was the third parent in every household. I listened to parent TV, who established my morals for the rest of my life. I listened to sister MTV, watching the countdown every New Year's Day of the top one hundred videos of all time. Parent TV was a liar; Sister MTV, the Goebbels machine for my generation. They whispered us to sleep with one-dimensional poems—recitations on what to dream, who to be, what to wish for.

If those were the years, Mr. President, that you'd turn the tide of history away from totalitarian darkness and into the warm light of the future, why is everything now so perpetually dark? Why am I jumping off the platform at 9:03 onto the warm sunlit tracks below?

Something's missing in the city's sky. Something is wrong. We are in a rapid descent. We are all over the place.

O, O, O, a nation mourns her fallen barbicans, her pillars of progress. There are moments in history when time folds, disappears; there are moments in history when time obliges no more sense. It's 9:03, and I am dying. If it were 8:46, it still would be the same. The time's inconsequential—the neglect and the loss are what matters.

The downtown skyline awakens from the rays of the rising sun. Something's missing. Something is wrong. And I remember they were torn asunder, duel dream gone mad, confederate dream of union proved false again. Me and You; Me as You; we too were torn asunder. And out went forth the cry—O, O, O, a nation mourns her fallen barbicans. 8:46, 67°, 8:46, 19c.

The water recedes; Brooklyn with it recedes, until it's completely gone, and I circumnavigate my eyes back to the city that is about to swallow me; but now I'm watching a boy, watching him from below and feeling him from inside. He's staring out the window of a subway train as it descends, DEK, TETRiS, MUTZ, rN, AVOID, AVOID, AVOID, dROId past the buildings of the Lower East Side into the tunnels. I look into him: (I am falling) and I realize I'm looking around at myself; and I see into him: (I am falling) and all he wants, all he needs, is to get home to something that he defines as best he can, vaguely, as a dream.

And the dream it seems has faded by the wear and tear of all the years.

The darkness it seems has settled.

The harvester had sowed a beautiful harvest that somehow reaped and garnered empty.

PHaMe, IRaK, ha, BeL, CHiP., HCE, SOaK, ZAR, BOO, BOO, dark dark dark dark dark, RK, DEK, OH!, OH!, PHaMe, HCE, ligggght, VON, CANAL ST., CANAL ST., CANAL ST.: checking out some kid: cute—on vacation with his parents. Mom and dad sit by me. His sister checks me out. I just glare at her brother. I imagine my mouth on his cock; imagine pulling that blond hair as

I fuck the shit out of his mouth; imagine the smile on his face as I lift his legs high in the air and pound away so hard that tears start pouring down his soft young skin. He holds a book in his hand. "9/11 In Remembrance. The Story of the Twin Towers." O, O, O, a nation mourns her fallen.... I see dead water girdled by the tracks into a trench, fetid streams littered with decay, CAUTION RODENTICIDE.

The tracks are gleaming like silver blades under the risen sun. I am hearing the train approach. Look up—Smith-9 Streets....

We had been eyeing each other for a couple of days. I had tried to kill myself, and everyone made it out to be this really big deal. I remember being on the F train and just watching the world of lower Brooklyn pass itself below me, a neglected land full of American refuse. I looked at all those houses that stretched eastward, the Jewish houses of Midwood, beyond them a glimpse of the houses of even richer Jewish Ditmas Park; and all those rooftops below the F train tracks on MCDONALD AV, which marked the boundary between rich and poor, with their various cries for help—MUTZ, BBB, StaRZ. I imagined lost children climbing up to the rooftops and flying high to unreachable places, like Peter Pans in the middle of the night, just to tell the world that they too are alive; that past the magazine stands and the large ads of airbrushed gods that loom high above us everywhere we go there was a real New York, a passionate New York; that beyond all of the plastic and underneath all of the neon glare and multi-colored light, there was still a humanity in New York City, ACiD, MUTZ, U CANT STOP ME, CANO, LITE, dOOR, CAST—*zoom zoom zoom* goes the train, *zoom zoom zoom*—and then the graveyard stretching eastward and westward of MCDONALD AV, the world of the dead that cares not for things like the established boundaries of neighborhoods called Midwood and Bensonhurst or for the fabricated partitions of economic emotions called wealth and poverty. The world of the dead is the world of the dead; the living don't figure in. It was like its own city, yet another city within this city of a thousand cities, that cemetery.

It's 9:03, don't be afraid—Jump.

Somewhere in my life I'm falling.

I am…

falling.

I got to my mom's after that train ride. I walked along SURF AV watching the rides as they prepared themselves to sleep away the upcoming seasons. I heard the screams from the CYCLONE and "BUMP BUMP BUMP YOUR ASS OFF."

I walked into her apartment with a sigh, said hello to the figure in front of the TV, walked to the drawer on which my young mother stared at me from a fifty-year-old black and white photo. I looked down and saw a bottle of Ambien in my hands. To be or not to be, to see or not to see, to live or not to live, to give or not to give. To cherish or to sell. I took four, just to sleep, and opened up *Ulysses*:

Sleeping sickness in the air. Walk on roseleaves. Imagine trying to eat tripe and cowheel. Where was the chap I saw in that picture somewhere? Ah, in the dead sea, floating on his back, reading a book with a parasol open. Couldn't sink if you tried: so thick with salt. Because the weight of the water, no, the weight of the body in the water is equal to the weight of the. Or is it the volume is equal to the weight? It's a law something like that. Vance in High school cracking his fingerjoints, teaching. The college curriculum. Cracking curriculum. What is weight really when you say the weight? Thirtytwo feet per second, per second. Law of falling bodies: per second, per second. They all fall to the ground.

Someone called. The phone kept ringing. I took ten more pills, and in the midst of it I wrote what the psychiatrists would later call a suicide letter. A tired hand on ivy paper, in black ink: "PERMANENT VACATION."

Twenty more pills and Sonic Youth's blaring from the speakers and you're holding my hand as we walk barefoot along Annandale Road and my father chasing me out of the house with a knife and Josh telling me he loves me and coke and coke off of cocks and cocks off of coke and I thought he really loved me, MADR MADR MADR, and the whole world that was and the whole

78

world that might have been and the whole world that never was:

Jehovah, collector of prepuces, is no more.

Of course, I woke up. They told me that I had taken "approximately 300 mgs of Ambien." I "got out of bed, turned on the bath, and let the water flood the house" as I "sliced away" at my left wrist. My "mom rushed into the bathroom"; she saw me standing in an impotent red ocean that refused to cease to flow. She called out my name. I turned around. I was in a bloodstained towel. I "couldn't turn the water off." I "couldn't stop slicing" my arm. I "couldn't speak." The whole place was flooding, blood and water all the same. I remember a bottle of pills floating in the deluge and then I remember vague images in the Hospital and my first clear sight was Frankie. He was tall. He had blue eyes. He smiled across the table.

We had been eyeing each other for days until Frankie came up to me and said, "So they finally got you off CO?" (CO was the abbreviation the psych. ward used for Constant Observation.) "Yeah." He sat down. We talked; became friends. He knew what I was in here for; but I had no idea why he was here, so I asked.

"Same shit as you." He turned over his left arm and there were raised lines that stretched from one corner of his wrist to the other.

"Wow! That's a deep cut."

"Yeah, I was on a lot of Zanax when I did it. I was taking a bath and I just sliced away."

He looks up at me. His eyes are wild, full of fire, beautiful and big and strong.

"Who called the Hospital?" I asked.

"I did. As soon as I started to see that blood flowing, I freaked, you know, and I got on the phone and they brought me here. I got up and stumbled through my house, the shit flowing out of me like a red river."

"Were you scared?" I asked.

"Scared, fuck no! I was still high the first two days, so I had no idea what the fuck was going on, but that third morning, I woke up, and I was like '*shit.*'"

"Yeah, I can understand. There's that fucking moment where you are like *shit*. I thought I was dead, and this was Hell or something, you know?"

He laughed. "It's not Hell. It's just life."

He stared at me, fumbling with his long fingers.

"So how'd you do it?" he asked.

"Ambien," I said, plowing my spoon into my peach pudding.

"Fuck, man—that's the worst! Didn't you know you sleepwalk on that shit?"

"Do now. I got up and almost flooded my apartment."

Someone walked in and told him that he had a phone call.

"Listen, I'll be right back, OK? You'll still be here?" he asked.

"Yeah, I will."

Ghosts. Ghosts. Everywhere I go there are pieces of you. A life composed of ghosts.

Frankie and I became really close, really fast. He was only there for three more days because he had called the ambulance himself. My punishment was to be longer. They were going to have me there for at least two weeks. Fuck it, I thought. I began to make friends, and I got food and meds, and everything began to look all right.

Frankie used to have a girl who'd come to visit him during visiting hours. I eventually got around to asking him who she was.

"Oh, she's my ex-girlfriend. I can't stand the bitch. I walked in on her one night fucking some other dude. Wanted to kill them both."

"Then why does she come and visit?"

"'Cause we got a two-year-old girl together."

Frankie, the twenty-two-year-old kid from Bensonhurst, so beautiful it was hard to imagine that such a thing could be, had a two-year-old girl. That means that when I was finally graduating from Bard having loved you for four long, hard, and terrible years; when I had seen the image of myself shattered by the indifference of your expression; when I finally began to accept how ugly you really were, letting the frost begin to settle on my heart, to the south of us a kid named Frankie and a girl were fucking—no, making love—in a room somewhere in the neglected areas of New York City, and from that love would be born a child. Frankie at twenty-two now has to deal with fatherhood.

Although his life had been hard, Frankie wasn't a destroyed person. He radiated an energy that proved the existence of something that might be called a God.

Frankie lived with his mom, too. It didn't bother him. On the other hand, living with my mom tore me apart. The last night he was at the psych. ward, we were talking. It turned out that Frankie was a graffiti writer.

"You ever write on the N line?" I asked him.

"What, you mean when it goes outside? Yeah. But I usually do it along the F line. The N line's too crowded, and I don't wanna write over anyone. But yeah, fuck, I've written there a lot. Have you ever seen MUTZ?" he asked.

"Yeah, of course!"

"That's me. I'm MUTZ."

"That's so fucking funny! I've written about you."

(I pass your name all the time. Nameless name now made human.)

"Yeah, in what?"

"I write stuff, and a lot of it is just graffiti on paper." I paused, nervous. "Can we write sometime when we get out of here?"

"Yeah, sure. I'll give you my number."

The next morning Frankie came into my room as I was reading *Ulysses* and handed me a piece of paper. There was a faint trinity of light rising from the window into the doorway. He stood there, his beautiful body sliced momentarily in three.

"This is my mom's number, and this is my cell

number," he said. "Call me when you get out. We'll figure something out."

I followed him to the elevator to see him off.

"Don't forget what I told you," he whispered on his way out. "Just tell 'em what they wanna hear. Be all smiles, they don't give a fuck. They just wanna believe that you're OK. They just wanna believe what they wanna believe, man. And that goes for outside too. People are fakes; pretending's the best way to get them off your back."

There are many kinds of love between people. Frankie knew I was gay. For all I knew he could have been too. But when I thought about him, it wasn't sexual. I guess if it was anything, it was spiritual, kind of the way children think of stars or the sky or each other or themselves. Kind of the way children think period, in thoughts without boundaries. After Frankie left, I began to think that in a lot of ways he was the better version of you. The only difference is that you walked through the world as a beautiful boy with a heart and soul that were as spoiled as America itself; and Frankie, for all his Brooklyn boy badness, for all the shit most people would have thought of him as he walked along the streets of New York, was really kind.

America has forgotten how to love. It's grown up to become everything it had hated as a child. It's grown up to be exactly like the parent from whom it once had run away. America dreamed of the day it would get a Frankie. Frankie was the goal of that pioneering rebel, who, as a child, despised the world around him, which was filled with people exactly like you. America has found her Frankie; and she put him away in the psych. ward at Coney Island Hospital, far from the large house and the privileged life she proudly put aside for you.

I never did call Frankie.

After the constant observation was over, they moved me into a room with a kid named Jose Menendez. Jose was a recovering heroin addict and a recovering crack addict; and for the first two days, he lay in bed trying to get rid of the shivers. The Hospital was helping him out with a heavy dosage of Methadone, but the Methadone's effect looked like it was just keeping him alive—barely. He spent most of the first day rolled up in a corner, covered in sheets, slowly coming back to life. It was a slow and useless resuscitation.

Jose had gone through it many times before.

They'd bring him in somewhere—jails, detox clinics, psych. wards—and do their best to keep him alive. After their best had been accomplished, they just left him alone. I guess as far as all these places go, all these places filled with people screaming Right to Life, breathing Right to Life, bombing life for Right to Life, the definition of a life is simply to keep the asshole going. Seems a sort of a joke. Read your own obituary notice they say you live longer. Gives you second wind. New lease of life: and then again forgotten.

When I first met Jose Menendez, I got really nervous. He looked like a crook and seeing him huddled in the corner like that brought out a reaction that afterwards I'd realize was a reaction of American instincts: Jose Menendez was a Hispanic New Yorker; he was a heroin addict with the shivers huddled in the corner of a psych. ward at the very bottom of Brooklyn; and my immediate (and natural) American reaction was to watch out for this kid. For the first two days, I counted the seventeen dollars I had hidden in my pocket to make sure he didn't get to it. Having been an American all my life, I was hardwired to judge this small curled-up creature as a bad sign. I know all this now, because by the time Jose left the ward, his stuff thrown quickly into a fresh black garbage bag, I began to love Jose—love him as a human being.

As the days wore on, Jose and I became friends. I stopped going to bed at nine o'clock after medication and started staying up and talking to Jose until midnight. I learned that what kept Jose going was his wife, Maria.

During Jose's last stint in an upstate prison, Maria smuggled in heroin for him. When he got sent upstate, he was already an addict; and without the junk he became weak.

"Prison's not a place where you want to be weak, man. You always wanna watch your back, fuck that shit man, you always *need* to watch your back 'cause you never know when a nigger's gonna pull out a blade or try to slice you or some shit like that, you know. So I couldn't see because I was thrown in there and they ain't got any medication windows Upstate. No one's giving you Methadone because you need that shit to stay alive. I couldn't see, man, and the worst thing in prison is not being able to see."

So Maria began bringing Jose his heroin, and all of a sudden he could function again. On her last visit Maria got caught. Jose was supposed to be getting out in a week, and she came to provide him with what he needed to make it through that last week. The State of New York sentenced her to two years upstate.

I used to watch the Empire State Building from the Activities Room. I'd stand there, the mumblings of the hidden and forgotten going on behind me, and watch that tower from the gated windows, past the leaves and the trees and then all of Brooklyn, rise up like a never-ending erection; and what got me through the days was knowing that when I got out I would be new, I'd be fixed, I'd be like everyone else, and I'd be a fireball in my new and improved condition. I'd take that city by storm: I still wanted it, fame and power and money; and all Jose wanted to do was figure out a way to get upstate and see his Maria.

I wonder what Frankie's dreams looked like and felt like when he slept on his bed at Coney Island Hospital's psych. ward.

I wonder what Jose's dreams looked like.

I wonder what my mom dreamt of at night, what colors she saw, while I was half a mile away imprisoned doubly now, by aging walls and by my own self, aging too.

As far as I remember, I had no dreams when I stayed at the psych. ward. I just slept a lot, pretending I had accomplished what I had sought out to do, until the medication began to work and forced me to realize that my Ambien suicide had failed. I was alive; and this time, I wouldn't get on that wheel. I'd stay away from it. But still I watched that tower, always on my mind, that great American tower; and still I had the same towering thoughts; still the American dream cast its heavy shadow down upon my life. Maybe the tower is all I dreamt of while I slept in my bed at the Coney Island psych. ward. Maybe I dreamt of its whole life from its beginning to its end, like the vision in Andy Warhol's "Empire" extended for the whole life of the building and separated neatly into a two-week period of some boy's forgotten dreams.

There were others too that I remember.

There was Jessica, the twenty-two-year-old Catholic schoolgirl who had never done a drug and one night ordered seven grams of cocaine and did them pile-by-pile in the span of an hour. Cocaine is usually a slow suicide; but Jessica, never having touched the drug before, thought she might as well save her time and money and do it all in one shot. She was pregnant, and her parents wanted her to have an abortion—even though that went against the standards of their Church. But Jessica was resolved to keep the baby because it was her baby, and it was her decision what she would do with it. Not her parent's. Not her State's. Not her Church's. When she asked me what I thought, "you know, about the baby," I told her that "it's always a good choice to keep your child alive."

And there were the Invisible Nurses, who'd flicker from their nowhere into the corners of our eyes—transmute themselves through tiny drops in the feel of needles pricking—so that when our eyes would finally arrive to view the place where we were startled, *they* were already inside—*attacking from within, collapsing the eyelids, collapsing.*

And there was Beth Griffen, who the Invisible Nurses called "schizophrenic," but who was actually a woman simply living in another world outside the dimensions of our standard conceptions of time. And we'd always meet the dusk together sitting on the benches by the wall—and I stare out through the barred-and-gated windows as the collapsing hours punctuate her speech: "Yes, because he never did a thing like that before—(and the last time he came on my bottom). I know what boys feel: 'Imagine I'm him.... think of him.... can you feel him trying to make a whore of me?' There's nothing like a kiss, long and hot, down to your soul.... almost paralyses you. I wonder, was he satisfied with me? I wonder, is he awake thinking of me or dreaming, am I in it?—That thunder!... As if the world was coming to an end!... I thought the heavens were coming down—thunderbolts!... What could you do if it was running and rushing about? Nothing! Always with a smell of children off her—

Nigger!—Jesus Jack, the child is a black—falling over one another. There's something I want to say to you—falling, one after another.... to extinction... such a long one, so cold and windy—I think I saw his face before somewhere. (Kiss me straight on the brow and part—which is my brown part!).. Forget it. God only knows. The skin underneath is much finer, where it peeled off—there, on my finger; it's a pity it isn't all like that. (Yes, I think he made them a bit firmer, sucking them like that so long—he made me thirsty. 'Titties,' he calls them. This one, anyhow, stiff. I'll take those eggs, beaten up with marsala, fatten them out for him—what are all those veins..?; curious, the way it's made with his two bags full, and his other thing hanging down out of him or sticking up at you like a hatrack.).. and I was selling the clothes and strumming in the coffee palace.... (This one not so much; there's the mark of his teeth still, where he tried to bite the nipple. I had to get him to suck them, they were so hard. He said it was 'sweeter, and thicker, than cow's... milk me into the tea....' An hour he was at them, I'm sure. O Lord, I wanted to shout out all sorts of things—'Fuck!...' 'Shit!...' Anything at all... 'Ugly!)..' the tumbling, (and my tongue between my lips). Frseeeeeeeefronnnng, train somewhere whistling! Old sweet sonnnng, the poor... out all the night... and the smell of the rainwater—(Regards to your father Captain GroveXXX)—those poor horses... it's like all through a mist, makes you feel so old. What age was I then, the night of the storm? I used to be weltering then; in the heat, my shift drenched with the sweat stuck in the cheeks of my bottom—on the chair; when I stood up, they were so fattish and firm—when I got up on the sofa cushions—to see with my clothes up—and the bugs, tons of them!... Didn't I cry? Yes. We're never easy where we are: the same old reveille in the morning: the days like years. Not a letter from a living soul, except the odd few I posted to myself with bits of paper in them.... So bored sometimes I could fight with my nails. Now with the hands hanging off me—the window!... (Aren't they thick—never understand what you say even. You'd want to print it up on a big poster for them.).. Love is sighing. I am dying. My goodness, there's nothing.... throw you out in the bottom of the ashpit. He put his tongue in my mouth; his mouth was sweet-like.... young. I put my knee up to him. Yes, O, yes: I can see his face—Frseeeeeeeeeeeeeeeeeeeefrong, that train again... weeping tone. (No man could look at my mouth and teeth, smiling like that—and *not* think of it! My hole is itching me always, when I think of him.) I feel some wind washing every bit of myself—back, belly, and sides. Sweeeee—there's that train.... far away. Goodbye to my sleep. Hear him falling up the stairs of a morning; and the tide all swamping in, floods in through. 'There's no danger whatsoever. Keep yourself calm.' I suppose they're all dead and rotten. (I never came properly till I was what twenty-two or so—it went into the wrong place.) *She's* pretty, with her lips so red—a pity they won't stay that way! I was too, but there's no use going to the fair. I didn't sleep the night before. Sweet God, sweet God, when I'm stretched out dead in my grave, I suppose I'll have some peace. Yes, that thing has come on me, yes; now wouldn't that afflict you? Of course. Isn't it simply sickening? That night, it came on me—like that! O patience above, it's pouring out! Look how white they are! Nice cool pins and needles.—Everything connected with your glorious Body, everything underlined that comes from it.... disgusting you more with those rotten pictures children with two heads and no legs the old love is the new flirtyfying wait yes hold on this morning when I laid out softly sighs of love the light guitar where poetry is in the air the blue sea and the moon shining so beautifully theyre my eyes two eyes as darkly bright as loves own star arent those beautiful words as loves young star I often felt I wanted to kiss him all over also his lovely young cock I wouldnt mind taking him in my mouth nobody was looking with his boyish face I would too in a minute even if some of it went down what its only like gruel or the dew theres no danger what am I going to do about him I cant help it if Im young still rotten with disease O move over your big carcass the winds that waft my sighs to thee I suppose I oughtnt to have buried him in that little woolly jacket I knitted poor child but I knew well Id never have another our first death too it was we were never the same since O Im not going to think myself into the glooms about that any more.... the air of the night.... a noun is the name of any person, place, or thing.... what a pity he didn't stay. Let

91

me see if I can doze off.... one... two... three... four... five... what kind of flowers are those they invented?... like the stars... who was the first person in the Universe before there was anybody that made it all?... yes... the sun shines for you today, yes...."

I am falling, passing: the winds into the ponds; and a needle full of Ativan to stay our walk into the dusk.

The psychiatrists agreed: "Uh... the Invisible Nurses, uh, seem to be correct," they'd call in from their golf courses. "Yes. Molly's schizophrenic!"—"It's Beth, Doctor," "Beth. Molly. Who knows? Who cares?" And everyone listened as the doctors explained Beth away through schizophrenia, avoiding the blatant fact that there is a thin line and meager distinction between the schizophrenics and the geniuses of history.

"Heads or tails, my darling drear: heads you're schizo; tails, you're good to go."

And then there were all those drugs: "Klonopin," "Ativan," "Methadone," "Risperdal," "Prolixin," "Wellbutrin," "Lexapro," "Zyprexa," "Seroquel," "Lithium," "Celexa," and on and on all the way to the bloodstream—and all the way to the bank.

And all the doctors and all the therapists phoning in from long island tees.

"Um... tails!"

"Strap me first; then I'll strap you."

"Promise?"

"Would an NYU man lie?"

And all the police: "Have to hit you—doctor's orders."

And the guys who brought up our meals and had to yell "dietary" through the gates during feeding time.

And the silence that would meet them.

"Dietary!"

"Sorry, it's-a-schizo...."

"I guess an NYU man *would* lie."

"Dietary!"

"Risperdal the bitch!"

"Dietary! Are you people fucking hungry or what?"

"Yes... yes... yes..."

"Then open the fucking gate!"

But only the nurses have the keys, and the nurses are invisible.

And a couple of train stops away—Coney Island. And its ghettos and new condominiums and its beach that numbered millions in grains of sand and was nestled between the momentary roar of the old amusement park and the endless dancing of the ancient ocean, large, vast, beyond comprehension, the ocean, which New York, dead or alive, had slipped into and would slip into forever.

Two nights after my release from the Coney Island psych. ward: Dead or Alive blaring from the speakers.

"You're trouble," he says.

"Yeah, that's one thing you'll get with me—trouble."

I smile, sucking on a lollipop.

"What kind?" he asks, eyes moving to my lips.

"Depends," I say.

"Oh yeah, on what?"

He bites his lower lip.

"How much coke you got on you?"

He pauses.

"Coke?"

"Yeah, coke."

He smiles and then leads me, the sounds of the world disappearing behind us, into the dim light of a bathroom.

14 Street-Union Square. I step off the train onto the platform. So many people, but we're all alone. I run up the stairs, pass the decaying stone pillars, monuments for dead generations. Down the stairs—the 6 train is meeting me—I'm on it. I'm on it. So close.

I'm smoking outside with Jack. We're at the Bank, oh sorry, we're at *Element.* Jack's in drag as Sabrina looking like a cross between Andy Warhol and Tina Turner. I'm wearing my red Girl Scout hat, a pair of ripped jeans I stole from Jenna long ago, which I've pulled up to my knees, a pair of tube socks with holes I poked into them earlier, my Converse, and a tie. I feel the warm wind on my body; the boys keep checking me out.

We're smoking *outside* because it's illegal to smoke *inside*. "This bullshit makes me feel like I'm a child," I say to Jack as we move from the basement bend through the crowded dance floor above.

"Well, honey, that's e*xact*ly parental government."

Parental government and the blaring bright intrusive eye.

Twenty-four hour patrolled people.

"*Moth—er*, oh my god!" Two tall, pretty girls walk up to us. "Trannie realness. Mother, you are *the* trannie realness," one of them, the darker one, says.

Then she looks over and says, "Who is *this*?" moving close to me.

"This," Jack says, "is _____*."

"Hello, beautiful. I'm your Epiphany," she says.

She puts her arm around my neck, and my head ends up level to her breasts.

(My Epiphany tells me that she's on heroin and a little Methadone.)

"Nice," I say. "Heroin is fun."

"Yeah, but it's the Methadone that really feels good," she says.

"I'll bet. Well, you're set for the night, aren't you?"

"That depends."

"Yeah, on what?"

I feel something on my ass. It's the hand of my Epiphany.

Some guy comes up to me, starts chatting me up, tries to steal me away from my Epiphany, tells me, "I'm (*crackle, crackle, crackle*)," like it's supposed to mean something.

His eyelids are collapsing slowly. He keeps trying to keep them open. Open and shut, the lips of a pulsating pussy.

My Epiphany says, "I just want my lipstick all over that ass of yours."

I take a drag and smile.

Jack has gotten on top of a car (*cue static*) and is dancing to a music from some faraway place. (*Cue music. Play static.*) Some guy in sunglasses walks up to Jack. Snippets of the conversation hit my ear like broken glass falling from the sky, as I watch the guy—street level—and Jack—on top of the car still dancing—speak mutely. They seem to know each other from "the Max's Kansas City days." (*Stop static. Stop dancing Jack. Play music very low. Play static very low.*)

Suddenly, Johnny, gets the feeling, he's being surrounded by, ---ses, ---ses, ---ses, ---ses.

"Sure isn't the Bank no more," says Guy-in-Sunglasses—(coke alert coke red!)—looking at the building.

Jack takes a moment, then looking up at the downtown sky: "First time's a tragedy, second time's a farce."

(*Loud laughter from some unseen elsewhere. Cue-and-play-thunder-and-cue-and-play-crash. Stop static. Play music at full volume*): "Horses, Horses, Horses, HORSES, HORSES, HORSES, HORSES, HORSES...."

Somewhere in my life I'm falling.
There's a little place....
I am...
A place called space...
falling...
It's a pretty little place....
I am falling....
It's across the tracks, across the tracks....

A Polish boy is hanging on the other pretty girl, Acid Betty. I begin to try to get the Polish boy to take out his cock. My Epiphany joins in. The Polish boy is a pretty boy—skinny, nice straight brown hair cutting across his forehead. I begin to imagine him prone on an unknown bed. His jeans are pulled down to the back of his knees, and his white ass jerks around under the ceiling light of a New York City apartment. His face is buried deep in Acid Betty's crotch. Her skirts rest on her torso. She watches him coolly from a higher vantage point as he gorges himself on her cock.

"This kid looks like he'd take a good fucking up that little ass of his," (*crackle, crackle, crackle*) says, putting his hand on the Pole's ass, hardly able to stand.

My Epiphany tells him to shut up.

"Who's (*crackle, crackle, crackle*)?" I ask Epiphany. "He seems like a fucking prick."

She smiles, looking his way. "He is, but he's also this big time photographer, and he's good for some things."

"Yeah," I say, "like what?"

She looks down at me. "They don't just give Methadone out for free on the streets."

I point to the Polish boy—

"That boy's in love with your friend."

"Yeah, well, she's a good girl, and she'll definitely teach him a thing or two."

"About what?"

"Discipline."

"I wonder what his cock looks like."

"I don't really care about cock," Epiphany says. "Once you've seen a couple, you've seen 'em all."

"Yeah, and once you've sucked a hundred you've sucked them all."

"Oh, is that how it is?" she asks. "I wouldn't know."

"I'm sure you wouldn't."

She stares at me for a moment.

"So what do you do?" my Epiphany asks.

"What do I do?"

"Yeah, in New York."

"Well, I write."

"Really, what, like stories or novels...?

"No, nothing like that. It's kind of like graffiti on paper."

"*Paper* graffiti?"

"Sort of, but..."

"So you write graffiti?"

"Yeah, but not the way you think. I guess I call it graffiti because just like graffiti, it's raw and true.... kind of like a loud yell, that only some people can hear.... I don't know."

"I guess that makes sense."

She pauses.

"How do you make money? Are you a trust fund baby?— 'cause then I lucked out."

I laugh. "Far from it. Right now I'm waiting tables, but I'm quitting."

"So you're a waiter," concludes my Epiphany.

I stop for a moment and look around me. This lost nocturnal menagerie; these living ones attempting life. Now, my identity out, I feel like Clark Kent. I get sick for a moment, the days shadowing down on me. I think about running around that restaurant and sneaking peeks at the clock, hungover, depressed, worrying about drops of noseblood hitting bowls of soup as I place them on the table. I think about all those people traveling through, and me trapped here, another twenty-something-restaurant-statistic; and even though I'm standing above them, somehow, in my mind, I'm always on my hands and knees. Waiters are just legal whores.

I think about all those times I just stopped in the middle of the floor wanting to quit, no longer able to take it, and what kept me going? The call. The call to my dealer at the end of the night. I remember standing there, waiting for a bunch of losers to decide on which one they're going to put down their throats.

"What do you think is better...?"

Who knows, who cares? It all ends up as shit, lady.

"Oh, that. That's much better."

9:03. Five more hours, and then the coke reward. Break your teeth eating the rocks, and get to the surprise toy at the bottom of the crackerjack box. Tonight, I made two hundred dollars, already spent one-fifty on coke. I hate my job, but I love the pretense of myself; cocaine helps me get there.

I wonder how common it is, this dilemma/excuse. You can't be Superman without paying the price of being Clark Kent. "How do I buy the outfits," "how do I keep my body hot," "how do I get cigarettes and take cabs," and "how do *I* get that coke," that thing on whose rails I can ride into the lone phone booth in the secret corners, the only phone booth where you can become a superhero. I need the money.

She's smiling. "You do a good job pretending. I thought you were some rich kid, but you're just like the rest of us." She pauses. "You're just another whore."

I look at her. She's unraveled into the strokes and colors of my revulsion.

She blows a smoke-ring toward E HOUSTON ST.

"I told you I was your Epiphany."

23RD ST, 23RD ST, 23RD ST, 28TH ST, 28TH ST,...

Last night, the night just passed, its background music presented as a poem:

T'aint no big thing,
To wait for the bell to ring.
T'aint no big thing—the toll of the bell.
I grow addicted, spare for days,
Stroll downtown in the red light place.
Jump up, bubble up—what's in store?
Love is the drug and I need to score.

The train slows down. I can't wait to get out. I get up from my seat and walk to the door. As the 2ND AVE station announces itself in its planned beat of tiled signs, I put my sunglasses on. We walk up the stairs, and I tell David that yeah, I probably am hooked, that I probably am a cokehead. He doesn't say anything. We see a bunch of people outside, smoking.

I feel David tighten up.

"Hey, would you wanna take a walk around the block and smoke a cigarette?"

"Yeah, I would."

We turn around back toward E HOUSTON ST and then right. We light up and don't say anything until we're almost back on 2 AV. There's a construction site across the street with a few of its blue boards missing. There's a big bulldozer and a bunch of wrecked bricks covered in the faint light from a 2 AV streetlight.

David looks at me and says, "Hey, we should go over there and do a bump before we go in."

I look around, fearful a cop car could pass at any moment; but the place seems so dark and empty I decide

101

it's safe. So we cross E 2 ST, step onto the pavement and then off into the wasteland of the construction site. We walk across the jagged landscape, littered with its bricks and articles of trash from people who were here before— empty forties, crushed potato chips, a bag here, a bag there—(probably once held weed, big bags like that don't hold coke). We walk across this refuse sprinkled with soft light, which glows like unnoticed neon, and get behind the bulldozer. I take out a bag, and as I'm finishing it off some of the coke from the mound on my key falls to the ground like a small snowfall. I watch it sadly as it lands on a dirty newspaper page on which the word DARFUR is highlighted by a stray beam from the 2 AV streetlights.

We head to the Cock. As we enter, I see this boy, this beautiful young boy, slightly drunk, standing alone and smoking. I try to remember where I know him from, but I have to say hi to all these people while trying to keep my cool. Scott's doing the door, and he lets David in for free because he's with *me*.

"Wow!" David says. "Mr. Superstar! Remember when Scott wouldn't let you in without paying, no matter what?"

"Yeah," I say dully. "I remember."

I haven't seen David for so long. I wonder why the hell I even called him. I keep staring at that beautiful boy until I disappear inside.

The room is packed with bodies under a dark red glare, and the music hits me right away, *"Wooo-o catch that buzz, love is the drug that I'm thinking of. Baby, can't you see—love is the drug for me."*

Logan's supposed to be DJing tonight, but he'd never play Grace Jones. I push through the crowd to the DJ booth to see if it's Logan, but it's not Logan. It's Josh.

I walk up to him: his face is blank.

"Hey, it's me!"

"Yeah, I know," he says. "So what?"

He stares at me coldly for a second and then puts his headphones back on. I watch him for a moment, but I can't cry. I can't care. I can only be like you, and you can only be like me. Josh, we rode together that first time into the city over the Williamsburg Bridge. The Empire State Building was already a shadow. We had just been at my Greenpoint apartment getting ready, doing coke. You were so happy, and I loved you so much. You said, "We should go to the West Side Club together. We'll get a room and lots of drugs."

And I smiled, answering with excitement, as the image of a fuck fest orgy of pleasure crossed my cokey imagination, "That would be awesome!"

And you smiled and said, "I'll provide the entrance fee if you provide the drugs."

But now, it seems, we both are disappearing.

Someone's hand is on my shoulder. I turn around.

A million galaxies, and here we are. Doing what? Doing ourselves to death. Josh is ignoring me. How do two people go from youth high on coke entering the night like kids at the edge of a carnival to this—two tired shadows, no longer going into the night but always now within its nowhere, having been swallowed by it, having been swallowed by that Pacman on steroids, which is New York nightlife. Josh is so pale; no, that's me.

"Darling!"

I turn around. It's Joey: "Are you OK?"

Youth drowning, youth running away; we are so alive, but we die; in the expectant days awaiting, and in the arrival of their disappointing nights, we die hopeless.

"Me? Yeah, sorry... I spaced."

She looks at me for a second, studying what the problem is: "You sure you're all right?"

"Yeah, of course." I go to kiss her, one cheek, then the other: "You look gorgeous Joey, but when don't you?"

I try to force a smile.

"Oh, stop," she says, grinning and flagging her left hand. "You're the one who looks gorgeous. What's *this look*?"

I realize that I haven't taken my sunglasses off. Though they're good to hide in, sunglasses are a siren when you enter a dark bar. They scream: I'M FUCKED UP! I CAN'T HANDLE IT! HELP ME! I'M FALLING! FUCKING-HELP-I-CAN'T-HANDLE-IT-I'M-(crash-crash-crash-thunder)-FALLING-(crash-crash)-FUCKING-HELP-(thunder)-ME-(crash, crash)-I'M-FALLING!: and... *give it to me baby, got to have that drug, got to have that buzz, got to have that drug, got to have that buzz, got to have that drug, got to have that buzz....* "Oh, I *love* this song! I still remember one night when she performed this song at the Saint.... so long ago. You probably weren't even born."

"Yeah?" I say, deciding it's best to keep my sunglasses on.

"Oh, it must have been the early Eighties." She stops and smiles. "There was this queen," she laughs, "Oh— she was *a trip*! Her name was *Pootasa*. And that night she was trying to get with this kid who was a hustler, beautiful boy, much like you. And he walked away from her and she was," Joey laughs, "she was so *livid*—and I remember her yelling, as Grace Jones is on stage, 'You'll remember this day. One day I'll be a star, and you'll remember walking away from *Pootasa*.' And on and on about how this kid was a junkie, and the kid just— walked away." Joey pauses. "I wonder whatever happened to that kid." She freezes, imagining the possibilities. "My, was he beautiful." There's another pause, much colder; and she looks at me, searching for something in my eyes—but it seems that she can't locate what she had in mind.

"Excuse me, darling," she says in an unfamiliar voice, "I have to get a drink."

Everywhere I look, people I know. And everywhere I look, people on the outside—mostly boys hanging around and looking for something. The in-crowd and the masses, who give a shit about the in-crowd, who only care to get *themselves* fixed. Plain boys for plain boys. If they only knew that the in-crowd is looking for the same thing—the fix that'll fix what broke them, in that so distant and faraway past.

I'm in the bathroom with David. There are a bunch of other people there, but they might as well all be the same lost person. David sticks out only because he's talking to me, says something about having "read *Less Than Zero* finally," and then he asks, "What do you guys think it would be like to overdose? I mean to really overdose from this shit? Do you think it'd be better than *this*?"

He takes a keyful and snorts it up his right nostril. "Ugghhh, that is such a downer," someone says. "Yeah, · David—what the hell is wrong with you?" "Can you pass me the bag?" someone asks. "But I'm serious! I mean, I knew people who OD'd from heroin, like Stephen." "What's wrong with you? Why would you bring up Stephen?" someone asks. "Just because... it's creepy— this is what's eating all of us up, but no one ever dies from it." "Good, let's keep it that way—here you go darling...." "Snort." Pause. "Snort-snort." "Can we change the topic—please!" someone pleads, wiping his (or her) nose. "OK, OK. I was just trying to make conversation. *Touch—y!*"

Someone's written *Purpose is for losers* on the wall in black marker. I stare at the words. I let out a chuckle. It grows louder and louder. I'm laughing uncontrollably. The other seven people in the bathroom become silent. They're staring at me. They don't know what to do.

"I got away, yes I really got away. I got away, yes I really got away."

The wall's pressing against my back. *"MURDER!"* I'm sitting on the couch between the two bathrooms.

"*MANSLAUGHTER!*" I'm gone. "*All funded by, my tax dollar!*" I stay there for a bit and then I look over—two boys are making out. I don't care. I sit for awhile, still and falling. *Thirtytwo feet per second, per second.* People I know pass me, and they don't say a word. When I get so dark, so closed in, everyone avoids me. Anyway, it's getting toward the end of the night: they're all gone too. I look over at the two boys—I can see the frail red light hit their faces. It's my angel from outside. I interrupt him: "What's your name?" He looks annoyed: "Alex." He tries to go back to the other boy's lips, and I stop him on the periphery: "You're beautiful." He ignores me, moving his pink lips, maliced by the bar's red light, to the pink-red lips of the other boy.

He's so close to me.

I can feel the edge of his sweater brushing up against me.

It's Hell: to sit by you as you kiss another boy.

It's Hell: the boy you're kissing looks over and whispers something about, "Your boyfriend doesn't get the hint."

It's Hell: my angel doesn't even turn around. He just mumbles, "Who cares?" between the kisses.

The kisses.

The kisses within the red light hitting their soft innocent faces. They too are decaying. I was once like them, and now I'm *this*. In-crowd, out-crowd, the night doesn't care. It will swallow all of that desperate and homeless generation, which is my own, swallow us all alive. It will unhinge us from the marvel of yesterday's boys and girls to pour us bitter down onto the shadows of tomorrow. The wall's pressing against my back. I'm watching them. The wall's pressing against my back, and I'm watching them. The wall's pressing against my back, and I'm watching them kiss, and I realize that kisses have been exiled from my life.

David comes up to me and says, "Hey, we gotta go. The lights are already on." He's right. I look over—the two boys are gone. Most of the bar is empty. David helps me up. We do one more bump in the bathroom. On my way out, some black girl I don't know stops me and says, "Oh my God, you look just like Michael Alig!"—(which I don't).

"Do I now?" I ask bitterly.

She doesn't catch the bitterness. She's too high and happy.

"For sure."

"Did you know Michael?" I ask her.

"Did I know Michael? *Girl*, we used to *party-it-up* at the Limelight together."

"Great." I say and start walking away.

"Wait!"—she grabs me—"Are you the new Michael Alig? Did you come to save us all?"

I look at her face. A huge grin spreads from cheek to cheek; there's a psychotic, fanatic desperation in her eyes.

I pull my arm away from her. "No, I'm not the new Michael Alig, and I'm definitely no one's savior."

We walk out the door, and David says that she was a "total nut."

I don't respond.

"So what are you gonna do?"

I look around for Alex, but I can't find him. There are other boys, still dreaming homeward possibilities, but I'm tired of substitutes.

"I'm going home."

"You can sleep over if you want," he says.

"No thanks," I say and begin to walk away.

"I'll see ya," he yells after me.

I'm the only one on the F platform. I begin to think about that fanatic at the end; and I remember Michael's song. Money, Success, Fame, Glamour. The addiction of a new American generation. No, I'm not your Michael Alig, but Michael *was our* precursor, *our* predictor, *our* presenter. Precursor, predictor, presenter of what would come. Money, Success, Fame, Glamour. An angel's body dismembered, boxed up, and then dumped in the Hudson River by four hands chilled through fourteen days of heroin, twenty fingers frosted by fourteen nights of cocaine. I guess angels never could exist on Earth. Either they're slaughtered physically, or prove themselves false by opening their mouth, by speaking and acting against how you dreamed they would. "Are you the new Michael Alig?" she asked desperately. Well, what did Michael, the Archangel, do? He precursed, predicted, and presented a generation full of me's and you's, who live out their night-day nights and their day-night days as only me's, or only one me. Who can save you, desperate and fanatic, four-a.m.-girl? Who can save you when no one else exists but you yourself, when all you know is "me"? "Are you the new Michael Alig?" What, what did he, Michael, the Archangel, do? All he did was precurse, predict, and present what we, the children of the eighties, would become: famished runaways searching for the bump in a land of plenty, searching for the hill that was promised us, searching for the city on that hill—but all we ever find is a flatlined plain. We are one big mass of a broken Me. We are a homeless mass searching for a home that never was and never will be again. We are a homeless mass of youthful flesh connected solely by addiction and nostalgia and a mutual collapse in loss and confusion. What kind of generation is that? That is a Generation Nothing. Don't be shocked, innocent parents of America, when my generation inherits this country and doesn't know what to do with it because no one ever taught us anything about it, this dream, this notion called America.

I imagine David as a Senator, Josh as a doctor, you as a priest, myself as a poet: and I see society crumble.

Yes, it was that Michael she so begged for, it was *he* that precursed, predicted, and presented what would become, and now is, you and me. But how could it have been any other way? A thousand dreams and a million commercials, and we find ourselves here, all grown up with no place left to go. And it's four in the morning, again.

I hear a rumbling. Then the silver film reel slowing down. I get into the train, "This is a Brooklyn-bound F train. STAND CLEAR...."

The fantasy I had of a bohemian night dimension everpresent alongside the machinery world of day has started to fade away like scattered sands from silent strands of seas so long ago, just after the passing of some forgotten storm. People come out for sex, which they hope will turn into love. And if they don't come out for that, they come to find adventure or escape or forgetfulness. And everyone is always hanging around, as long as the drugs are there, everyone is always hanging around, waiting, searching for that something that somehow got away. Everyone is trying to escape; everyone is looking to forget; everyone is gorging themselves on the waters of Lethe; and we are all choking. That's what it means to get fucked up. It's a collective choking into no tomorrow; it's an asphyxiation to the bottom of the sea.

The river of Lethe has filled with cocaine, heroin, television, sex, shopping bags of all colors in paper, plastic, reusable suede, beach bags heavy with bones, handbags sinking with tears—the river has filled with all the refuse we use to enhance our quality of life. The river is expanding. The river is overflowing. The deluge has arrived and covered our city upon the hill with garbage.

GRAND CENTRAL. "THIS IS GRAND CENTRAL." This is it. This is where I get off. I try to get up, but I'm clumsy. I've been sitting here for hours or days or years; and the coke has made me jerky, almost paraplegic. I

111

don't realize it until I try to get up and push through the crowd in the train. Where did all these people come from? Have they been here the whole time? Moving through the crowd, I see faces, some curious, others momentarily terrified, faces I have never known, faces with eyes that are sockets colored by various shades of the color spectrum. Nothing behind them. Nothing behind the color. I step onto the platform, and it really hits me now, how coked up I am. I take a seat and breathe a little. I need to calm down or I'll never make it up those stairs. There are too many people, too many dead people walking around really fast—briefcases and purses and business suits and suitcases all stamped D.O.A.U.S.A. Some black guy passes me and asks if I'm OK. "You doin' all right, bud? Need some help?" I take a deep breath in. "No." I tell him. "I'm just fine." I *am* fine. I'm going to see if love still lives. It's amazing how that all depends on one human being, on one train ride to a desolate town colonized into Poughkeepsie.

When I hit METRO-NORTH, I freeze. I have to buy my ticket and get out of here—fast. The clock reads 9:03. I look at the board to see when the next train is going to... three hours—the next train will be here in three hours. I missed the eight forty-six train. I missed the train to Poughkeepsie. I stand there not knowing where to go. Jack's? Coney Island? It's so late—or early. I reach into my bag for comfort. The letter's edge pricks my hand. I look up—and I see you.

I'm standing on the WEST BALCONY. I've been waiting for you. You had decided to come to New York to visit me. I was so ecstatic. It was the summer of our love, and I had waited, and then I saw you, your bare feet in those unlaced black boots and your jeans rolled up above the ankle, and I ran to you. I ran to you. But you weren't there. Later, you apologized, claiming something important had kept you in Boston. But you weren't there. You weren't there then, and you aren't here now, and your absence makes me feel like I keep being punched to the ground.

The letter's edge pricks me once more, reminding me of its presence.

I walk away really fast, my head down, tears in the corner of my bulging eyes, down down down, back into the underground.

The 6 train. Ding, dong. I step across the edge into the train and the doors close and the train makes its way south.

Totally different train.

Totally different direction.

Totally different,

From how I thought it was going to be.

I'm walking down the platform of the MONTROSE-AVE. L station. My body's still leaking all over the place, in the front, in the back. I check my jeans to see if they're wet, but I can't tell. I hate the L train because you're bound to see someone you know, and usually they'll check you out to see if you're still cool or to see how much you've fallen apart since the last time they saw you. I lick around my mouth and then spit on the tracks. A mouth full of cum definitely isn't the look.

Halfway through, sitting on the edge of his bed, he told me I'm HIV-positive. When I heard him moan in the late morning, I took his long dick out of my mouth and saw that it was spewing out jizz. I don't remember having any emotional reaction to what he said because I still hadn't come, and I was really high, and it was only four o' clock. Most importantly, there was still a full vial of coke we hadn't touched yet.

But when it was over, when I saw his face the way it really was, and his room the way it really was, when I felt his arms wrapping around me from behind, I got a little nervous. It's not that I give a fuck about dying, it's just that I don't want to die for him. I don't want to die for love.

I took a cab to his place because he said he'd pay for it. When I got there, I said, "hello," then went to the kitchen table where a half full vial was sitting by some lines. I did all the lines, then emptied some coke from the vial and continued. Line after line after line. He was trying to get the computer to work to play some music, and I kept going at the coke.

"Is this all we have?"

"Yeah, baby," he says coming up to me. He starts unbuttoning my jeans. He starts kissing me. "Should we get more?"

"Yeah, we should," I say, pulling away. "I'll call my dealer."

Twenty minutes later, his face is in my ass, and I'm pouring a mound of coke from the vial onto his flaccid cock. Inhale. Inhale. Go slowly on my cock, you tell me. Kiss the head, kiss the shaft. That's right, go all the way down. That's right.

"Swallow it down. Swallow it all the way down. That's a good boy."

I sit on your cock, let it fill me all the way. I wonder how dirty I am inside. I go up, your eyes go down. I go down, your eyes go up. You pull out and I lick myself off of you. From balls to head I lick myself off your cock.

Suck my dick, I tell you. I put on my Lynyrd Skynyrd hat and pull you by the hair up to the mirror. Lee Ranaldo is yelling through the speakers, *"I can't see anything at all, all I see is me. That's clear enough, and that's what's important, to see me."* I watch myself in the mirror as you suck my cock. I watch my thin body sweating, my blue eyes turning black, my face turning white. I pull your hair hard as I keep fucking you in the mouth with a limp dick that gets harder the more you work it with those pink lips of yours. *"My head's on straight, my girlfriend's beautiful, looks pretty good to me." Looks pretty good to me.*

Cocaine delivers me poorer and poor—
I am thurstin', I am thurstin' for more.

There's a part of me that hates you right now, another part that knows you hate me too, and what's left just wants to kill this thing called love. Somewhere, though, somewhere between all that, I believe that we know each other, and I believe that romance still has a chance. And right now, as I'm pulling your head back and forth with a violent movement onto my cock, this feeling, without location, without definition, as immeasurable and vast as the black space swimming between stellar bodies, is the strongest.

I spit on you. You spit right back. Really forceful like I'm useless and like you want me to know it. Then you go to kiss me. I kiss you back and then pull away to see your face. *All I see is me....* I SPIT RIGHT INTO YOUR EYE. For that I receive a hard slap on the face that makes my cock-ringed tumescent dick skip from the accompanying rush of blood.

The coke runs out. I go to sleep in your bed, and when you say, "Will it bother you if I stay up a bit?" I tell him, "No it won't bother me if you stay up a bit." Morning has come, killer of nightly things, reminder that we are nothing but the aging flesh of fragile days. He gives me a black mask to keep away the sun. As I pass out, I hear him say, "This place looks like a crime scene."

I wake up. Where are you? I'm at some boy's house. He's by my side. What's his name again?...

I told him I'd see him soon as I was walking out the door. Moments before, he rushed out of bed as I scrambled to get my things. He was right: the apartment *did* look like a crime scene. There were clothes everywhere, disrespecting the boundaries of adjacent rooms, cigarette butts in the sink, on the counter, in the multiple cups of lukewarm water, empty coke bags, empty vials, powder all over the kitchen table, his desk, his plates, and the mirror we took down sometime during the night. I decided to just focus my attention and gather the essentials, which will get me home, with the hope that everything else would somehow gather itself.

I hear a car honking its horn outside. "Man, these fucking cars! Either they take an hour to get here, or they come right away. No moderation."

Many times before, when I really needed to flee his apartment, it took three or four hassling calls to the Anonymous Car Service Company to get them to send a car fifteen minutes late. At those times, I was desperate; my eyes still round black globes, and my body still puppeted by the cocaine flowing around in my blood. At those times, I was desperate, like an animal tied with rope to a time bomb. I couldn't go outside and wait—no way—that would have been like stepping into another and dangerous dimension; but my patience for him and his apartment, the memory of him touching me and me touching him, weighed on my weak head and threatened to break it with every minute. I wouldn't be safe at these times until I got home and washed all of him off—his cum, his piss, his fingerprints. At those desperate times, the car was inevitably late.

But today, I was fine. I had already showered—alone—more to get the multiple layers of baby oil off my body than to get him off of it. He was right. The place looked like a crime scene, and we were its cadavers.

The car is green—they said they'd send a black one. A moment of panic: brief, but there. Even if I was fine and holding friendly flirtatious conversation, I didn't want to wait outside; and if this car was the wrong car I would be *forced* to wait outside, as mesmerized by fear as a deer trapped in the headlights. Yesterday, I marveled at how exposed the bedroom windows were. Nothing but thin transparent sheets covered them; and in the dark, all the lit up windows were like eyes, all focused on my naked body dancing around and my gesticulating hands, which moved along my ass cheeks as I performed a little dance. What if someone calls the cops and complains? What if they come and finally get me, before I even got to come. I scanned the morning horizon to validate those fears of last night, but it seemed the coast was clear. The coast is always clearer when your nerves aren't being fried by cocaine.

He was hard, and he was kissing me. I slightly and slowly returned the favor. For a moment, my lips hung on his lower lip, as if enticed by the erection, or disappointed for an instant by the inevitable ending of all things.

"You're all hard now. What a shame to leave."

"Give me a call sometime," he said, opening the door.

I always remember him—Kurt—because he looked much older in the day. He had these deep wrinkles around his eyes and his mouth, which gave his otherwise boyish appearance the brand of thirty-four years' living on Earth. That transformation from wet red hair dripping onto his gleaming torso as he sat in his chair, his dick hard—or limp, asking my lips to make it hard; that movement from a coked-out vision in the night to this one, just some HIV-positive guy in boxers holding the door open for me, managed beside my better understanding of it all to fill me with a soft disappointment. Last night, you were a fantasy. Today, you are real, too real; but this time I didn't think it for more than a second. I didn't think it as I looked at his tired face, or as I walked down the stairs. I didn't think it because I already knew it.

I already knew too well that the stuff of dreams is simply the stuff of dreams, and no one ever seemed to live up to the expectation. It's as if everything was too dead with the burden of age, too desensitized by all that's happened since our beginning, to anymore live up to the dreams dreamt by those who desperately and foolishly continued to dream the great dreams of the living. The wonder of my life, of all life, seeped away enough for me to know what a huge letdown this world really is.

Without another thought to him, I got into the green car—luckily it had been mine—gave the driver directions, and watched as the familiar sight of the decayed Williamsburg skyline whizzed by me on my travel southward into Brooklyn.

That night, I dreamt of Bard. It was raining, and I remember rushing in a car, and then running across a plain of soaked grass to a barn. A heavy thunderstorm pounded the Earth with warm rain. Inside, Emily was waiting for me. When we saw each other, we were so happy that we danced around in circles for a bit. Though it was night, and heavy with rain, an outside lamp cast the window's shadow perfectly onto the floor. I was late for something, but she had waited. It felt like graduation day, and we were graduating together. I'm filled with hope and sorrow as we twirl around. The beautiful chapter of my life that was Bard ends today, but another one—beautiful because it is unknown—begins.

And then I wake up. It was 9:03 PM that same day. The night had been the day, and the day had passed by again unnoticed. Here, Emily and I never graduated together; and Bard had been beautiful, but not the beautiful that flowed through me overwhelmingly in the dream. In my dream, the sorrow over beauty lost was the sorrow over leaving behind a perfect world, where I had been happy and free in the days and nights. In real life, the sorrow I remember upon leaving Bard was like the sorrow of leaving the funeral of a greatly beloved with whom a million words had been left unspoken. I sorrowed for Bard because I could never regain it and could never regain you; I sorrowed because I knew that the impossibility of regaining the dreams of my childhood, that the failure of those dreams, would eat at me until one day there was nothing left but the memory of dreams and how they fail when they are placed upon flesh. But here's the great question: if you don't place your dreams in flesh; if you disregard them when you see their potential in someone's eyes and someone's smile; if you look away because you know that, though the sparkle is there, the fire will not last long, because life sucks out the thunder and the flash really, really quick, then what do you do with dreams? If the world can't handle dreams where are they to go? Do they travel from bed to bed, from friend to friend, from place to place, and move on quickly after they have gotten all the little they could get? Or do they just stop, dry up, because they are tired of the inevitable failure; dry up, and with them, dry you up. For what else are you but the hope and the wish of your own dreaming?

"THIS IS 23 ST. THE NEXT STOP IS UNION SQ-14 ST."

Examples of Romantic Crime Scenes

Example Number One. I walk into his apartment. We had met once before at the Cock. I'm really high. I took a cab from Williamsburg. He has people over; and as I walk in, he's riding some guy's cock. There's another guy, a naked middle-aged man with glasses, who's watching or waiting or both. When he sees me come in, he unhooks the supine dick and introduces me to the guys, both of whom are drooling. I don't find either of them attractive; but seeing his naked body, I can't wait to have him to myself. He puts on shorts, and one of the guys puts his boxers on. "Can I talk to you in the bathroom?" I say.

We go to the bathroom. A single razor blade infringes on the purity of the sink's porcelain. I start kissing him and grabbing his big cock.

"Hold on, we have people over," he says. I tell him that I don't like them, that I didn't know they'd be here, that I only want him.

"So you want me to send them away?"

"Yeah," I say, kneeling down and licking his cock through his shorts.

"God, that feels good!"

He pulls me up. "I'll ask them to leave only if you let me fuck you for real this time." I agree. We walk out, and he sends the guys away. When they leave, I wrap my legs around him, and he takes me into the shower. He sticks a hose up my ass and the pressure really hurts. The water my ass spits out is full of shit. "We need to clean you up before I fuck you."

I met him at the Cock. I thought he'd be something different than he was. I try to avoid letting him fuck me all night; but finally, he forces me down and pulls my ass up into the air. "Not tonight boy. Tonight you're getting fucked."

He penetrates me, and I try to cut a line to kill the pain; but there's too much, too much pain.

Example Number Two. I met him at the Cock. He was tall and beautiful. I was wearing a Confederate flag, which I wrapped around my torso, and yellow American Apparel shorts. We made out against one of the pillars, and I really liked him.

"Let's go," I said; and as we turned left on Second and Second, he held my hand. He told me he was from San Francisco. He was drunk and happy, and I was high, and I wanted to suck his dick. When we got to his place, it turned out he didn't do coke.

"Mind if I do it?" I asked.

"Not at all."

He took off his shirt and pulled me into him to kiss him. I held onto his strong white chest, and then went down to lick his nipples, which were surrounded slightly by hair. His chest hair was minimal too; but at the bottom, toward the cock, there was an overgrowth of manly hair. It all made me very hot.

"I have to go to the bathroom," he said. "Why don't you take off that flag so you'll be ready for me when I get back."

I took off the flag and got on his bed with my sneakers and tube socks still on. I raised my ass in the air, pulled my shorts down, and waited for him. When he got back, he looked at the merchandise and said, "Nice. I like that. Turn around."

I did so. He was wearing a white robe, and I crawled to him and then stood on my knees. When he disrobed, he was fully naked, and I started to suck his cock right away. He had shaggy shoulder-length black hair. He kind of looked like you. Eventually, he wanted to sleep; but I kept sucking his cock anyway. I really thought I loved him. He asked me to let him rest, and I waited anxiously all night for him to love me again. Finally, after a couple of hours, I pulled down the sheet and started to suck his cock. It got hard fast, and then I raised myself and lowered my body onto it. He looked into my eyes the whole time, a meaningless and blank look. After he came he went to wash up, and while he was washing up, I jerked my cock until I came. We sat around his kitchen table for a bit, he in his robe, I in my shorts, and we had nothing to say. He made coffee. "I have to go to the bank," he finally said; so after we got dressed, we walked out together. I kissed him and told him to call. I really wanted him to, but he never did. I don't even remember his name; but for months, I hoped to run into him again. I never did.

Example Number Three. I'm lying prone on his bed, and he's lubing up my asshole. He tries to fuck me, but it doesn't work. I didn't like him, but I was desperate, and it was four a.m.

Example Number Four. Lying on his stomach, I stroked my limp cock. He was done, his cum on my face, the end result and epitaph to our long night together. I continued to jerk off, watching the porn on his computer. So recent a stimulus to our sexual fantasies, the images now flickered within the limbo of our bodies. "You'd like that cock in your ass. Shit, I wish there was another guy here to fuck you in the ass. I'd be in Heaven watching you get fucked by that guy while your mouth was wrapped around my cock."

And now his body was limp and tired. He got up to wash himself off; and when he returned to the room, I was still stroking my cock. Even I—yet unexorcised of the burden that had been heightened by all that crystal meth, with my balls still full of cum—even I could see the absurdity of my supine body, cock ring around my dick, trying to force an ejaculation in the midday light, which was breaking through the improvised curtains. I was going mad that this boy, who half an hour ago was fully involved in my body, who at one point in recent time was intent on the singular goal to press my body tight to his, who having been pulled into the demarcation zone of the night by his satisfaction and my frustration, was now surrounded by a cool detachment in the morning light, a detachment that made him unrecognizable. As I desperately stroked my dick, I noticed a large poster on the wall for "THE TEXAS CHAINSAW MASSACRE." In bold black type, the poster asked, "Who will survive, and what will be left of them?"

He came out of the bathroom fully dressed and watched me for a moment.

"You really have to leave now."

I missed the train to Poughkeepsie....

"THIS IS UNION SQ-14 ST."

I'm walking fast, eyes on the ground, to the N platform. When I get to the platform the Downtown side is sectioned off with yellow tape. Fuck, I think. Fuck, Fuck, Fuck, Fuck.

I look to the left—CAUTION THIS AREA HAS BEEN BAITED WITH RODENTICIDE ON 2-16-08, L To 8 Avenue & Brooklyn, and I see the stairs leading to the L train. I'll take the L. (That's L to the G—and then—take the F train home!) I run down the stairs passing scattered hipsters until I reach the back. I look at a map, mapping out my morning's journey. I started at 2 AV last night and ended up in Coney Island. (I trace my finger along the orange line.) Then I decided to go to Poughkeepsie, so I took the N. (My finger traces the yellow trail from Coney Island to 14 St-Union Sq.) I transferred at 14 St-Union Sq to the 6 train. (My finger traces the short green distance to Grand Central 42 St.) I pause, or sigh, or both at once; then my finger retraces the green path back to 14 St-Union Sq and I leave it there. On the map a big circle circumnavigates 14 St-Union Sq. The words YOU ARE HERE center the circle, and a large X in black Sharpie marker runs across the words and through the circle.

A Circle.
YOU ARE HERE
Where am I?
YOU ARE HERE
Where am I going?
X

November 8, 2000, around 2:30 a.m. I walk into the Campus Center. Crowds are spilling out from the multi-purpose room into the lobby. I nudge my way into the room, which is packed. On the wall, a large TV screen is relating the unexpected play-by-play of the election. It seems that something is happening with Florida. It seems that the Vice President is about to lose the election to the Governor from Texas.

I see you leaning against the wall, staring up at the huge screen, your eyes wide with excitement. I walk up to you, say, "Hi!"

You look down: "Oh, hey."

The results from Florida are announced. The Governor from Texas, it seems, will be our next President.

The room goes into an uproar. You're stunned.

"Are you OK?" I ask.

You awaken into scorn. "I think there are much more important things to worry about than how I'm doing. If I were you, I'd focus on worrying about yourself."

Hurt, I walk away, outside, onto a path that leads to Blithewood Garden.

The garden is empty, silent, still. The Hudson's waters are unmoved; the mountains are sleeping shadows on the other shore. A southbound train cuts across the river, not breaking the scene, but adding to it with reminiscences of a different time. He's right, I think: there are more important things to worry about. I turn around and head to my lonely room in the trailer, by the Old Ravine Dorms.

But he wasn't right. He, you, as was the case with most things, were wrong. Years later, as I was staring at the train tracks, I remembered that stab produced from that callous voice telling me *other* things were more important. Really? What's more important than our responsibility to those closest to us in our society. If we can treat the ones we're meant to love the most so coldly, what can we *expect* to receive from that mirror image of who we are collectively, which is expressed in our leaders.

Your comment to me that night only showed how much we as Americans deserved the Presidency of that Governor from Texas. The foundation of society, the day-to-day relationship of its citizens, had become so rotten, so uncaring, that it could only produce a monster at its head. Our generation, successfully indoctrinated by television culture, had been a silent generation. Those of us who spoke would prove our speech hypocritical by the ways we lived our daily lives. We treated people like we treated television shows—when the show was over, or we got tired of watching, we'd simply turn it off. We did the same with love, with friends, with our relationship to our own selves. We were captives of our upbringing. You expressed this newfound disability in humanity better than anyone I have ever known.

People are not television shows. People can't be turned off when we get bored with them.

Our greatest power politically is the way we handle our relationships with one another on a daily basis.

Our greatest failure politically is treating each other like we're all television shows.

We can't be monsters and expect leaders who will be saints.

We can't be gelded horses, and then wonder why, when bidden, we cannot bring forth life.

YOU ARE HERE. The L train slides slowly into the station. How long have I been here staring at those words, staring at that circle X-ed out with black marker? I get on the train. It's empty. "THE NEXT STOP IS 3 AV," and I look at the red lights to see what time it is. The doors close, and then the red lights tell me what time it is. It's 8:46 AM.

The first time I saw him, he was sitting in an empty classroom. He had long black hair, spiked in various places. He was wearing all black, and my eye caught his left wrist, which was braceleted with various pieces of string. Then I saw the X on his white hand. His hands were large and white and thin, and he had long bony fingers. I figured from the faded X that he must have been at the party last night, but I didn't see him. We must have missed each other. He was writing something. Then he looked up and caught me staring.

129

I saw two blue eyes. They looked calm and sad and curious, almost expressionless in their beauty and their curiosity. It was a face I had seen before many times. It was a face I had known, but only as air, as vapor, as feeling, a face that now took on the reality of form. It was the face on an angel, an old and ageless face written in the beautiful language of a young boy. His cheeks. His jaw. His forehead. His eyes. His nose. His eyes.

I quickly looked away and went into my classroom. It was Freshman Seminar, and our professor, Elisabeth Griff-Vance, had arrived. We followed her in loyally and excitedly. Elisabeth was a well-dressed, thin woman who sat herself in the horizontal center along the large table, taking a position sitting sideways, leaning against the armchair as if she were at a picnic posing for Manet. Very pretty. Later on, I learned Elisabeth was from French aristocracy and had been raised with all the privileges a young girl growing up in the sixties in such a position would have had.

"OK. Hello everybody. I am Elisabeth Griff-Vance, but my colleagues call me Etta. So I insist that you all call me Etta."

Some kids said hi, some said hello, some shook their heads, but everyone came to attention. We were sitting around the table, seventeen students, boys and girls, all eyes and thoughts on that pretty French thing leaning her meager weight on the unburdened wood of the chair.

"Everybody is good?" she asked. The class mumbled, almost in unison, varied agreements that, yes, everyone was good. Some kid made a joke about how "could we be bad being in your class?" Alpha kid—he's going to be an annoying one to have to live through for the next few months.

"Well, thank you very much," Etta said, smiling. "OK. And now to business." She paused. "I presume we have all read *Beowulf.*" She paused, smiled. "Yes?" she asked, looking around the room flirtatiously after having received a lukewarm response.

"Yes," the crowd said in unison. Seventeen as one. (Well, almost.)

"Good. Well, today, we will discuss this great classic of our Western heritage, and then the real fun begins. For our next three sessions together we will be reviewing the language in which the original work was written, and then you will be ready to read a whole section in the original Old English—like the true scholars you will have become."

Some smiled. Some didn't care. I stayed in my corner trying to hide. I hadn't read it—not this time. I skimmed through it because I spent most of the week drinking and hoping to find a boyfriend.

The discussion began, and the Alphas of the class, the real go-getters, the mamma's and papa's boys and girls who came here to make something of themselves, chimed in with their pointless opinions.

I wonder what class he's in. I wonder what he's doing, how he's behaving, what he's thinking. Have I crossed his mind, even briefly, from curiosity? Well, I'm already marked in one way or another on his mind. I wonder if I'll stay. I wonder what his name is.

Hello. "Hello. The boy in the corner—what's your name?"

"Me?"

"Yes, you, off in la-la land. What is your opinion?"

"My opinion. Of what?" I asked

Laughter. The Alphas look down and shake their heads. Etta does not look pleased.

"Your opinion *on* the question I just posed." She paused, watching me; "Which was," she says looking away, "to refresh those minds momentarily absent from our classroom," then back at me: "Do you think that Grendel is treated fairly in the work?"

All eyes move to me. My shoulders raise uncomfortably to my ears. Grendel. Know the story. Studied it in high school. Grendel's the monster. Beowulf kills him and his mother.

"Well," I began, "I think that it's interesting that as far back as the time of *Beowulf*, mankind has celebrated conquering the darkness present in his existence, which Grendel and his mother, to me, represent."

Good start. Etta's smiling. You're on a roll. Keep going.

"It seems," I continued, "*Beowulf* is just an introduction to a theme that will plague Western literature from there on."

"Oh," Etta says dramatically, moving her right hand to her chest.

132

She has small titties, but they fit her well.

"*Plague*—what a strong word," she says to the class.

Smiles. The Alphas laugh and shake their heads.

"Well, what is this theme that will *plague* Western literature, if I may ask?" Etta says, moving her eyes back to me.

The other sixteen pairs of eyes follow. Boy, she likes that leaning pose. She'd look great smoking a cigarette! I wonder if she smokes. Probably Capris, or something like that. Long and skinny, emasculated white sticks.

"That theme?" I pause. "That theme, which plagues Western literature and mankind," I pause, thinking, "is... *fear*!.: the fear to look at man's other self, man's darker self, his deeper self. The self that knows no bounds because it is moved by one force only, the force of hunger. We seem to be afraid of a side of us, which *is* us, and connects *us* to our own pasts. We call it ugly or bad or evil. We demonize it and make it take the form of monsters. But it's always there. It takes the form of our shadow, that other, darker self, that Grendel of ours, and our shadow lives as long as we do, and our shadow is made of darkness."

Bam. That was awesome! Well done.

The classroom is silent, all eyes now fully on me. I wonder if I pulled it off. I can't tell, because Etta's just staring at me, into me, trying to make out whether it's bullshit or real. I myself don't know where that came from—a talent, I guess. I watch Etta, and the classroom seems to wait for her response; and then it comes—a smile which breaks slightly at the sides of her thin lips, and then grows into a curved red line, painted with the utmost care.

"It seems," she says still looking at me, "we have a poet in our midst. Yes." She pauses, and then says seriously, staring at me intently, "Brilliant, this is very, very brilliant." I can sense a disappointment among some of the kids, but I'm just happy I got away with it. "You have brought up issues and concerns that could be the basis of a whole course! Very good." She smiles, turns away, and then to the rest of the classroom, "What does everybody else think about what your colleague has said? Are we afraid to look into our darker selves? Is Grendel treated unfairly by the unknown author of *Beowulf*?"

I wonder why that X was still on his hand. Didn't he shower? Black marker *is* hard to get off though, and it *was* faded. I wonder if he had to run this morning, had to run after spending the night with some boy, maybe a boyfriend. Was that why he was deep in thought? Was he thinking of love? If so, it looks like a love gone or going wrong.

Man, he is beautiful!

The discussion heats up, led by the Alphas, who seem to be on the attack. Good citizens in the making. I'm left alone for the rest of it, so I just keep thinking about that X on his arm. How could I miss him last night? Still pretending I'm straight. I must have been too busy showing off, making out with Rana or whatever her name was. I wonder if he saw that? He probably thinks I'm a jerk. And what about all those bracelets made of various pieces of material around his wrist? Then I hear Etta say, "OK, unfortunately we must get down to a more difficult business now, though many of you have brought up wonderful points. I am satisfied that you are now ready to attack the material in its original." She pauses, opening up a book and gently turning the pages. "Open up your Old English textbooks. We will go through some words together so that it might be easier for you when you are faced with these strange symbols on your own."

The grammar lesson begins.

Etta says a word. We pronounce it after her. She tells us its meaning. Then, we write it down in our books—its modern meaning beside it.

"Lidmann." "Lidmann." "Lidmann means sailor." Lidmann—sailor.

"Weccan." "Weccan." "Weccan means wake." Weccan—wake.

Some girl raises her hand. "Professor Griff-Vance, does waken mean wake up, or is it like a wake?"

"Good question. We will get to these difficulties later on, but very good question...."

"Denise."

"Yes, excuse me. I will learn all your names—in time." She laughs. "Let's continue."

"Mor." "Mor." "Mor means wasteland." Mor—wasteland.

"Morgencolla." "Morgencolla." "Morgencolla means morning horror." Morgencolla—morning horror.

Etta looks at her watch. "Oh no, I'm sorry, we have gone over our allotted time. So, for next week please learn as much as you can in the first blah blah blah."

I gather my things and rush out. I look into his classroom, but it's sterile, the way classrooms at Olin Hall always were when they were empty. His chair is empty too. It has been moved slightly out of place, probably when he got up to leave.

He left. You left. You're already gone.

Well—when I see the price you pay, I don't wanna grow up. I don't ever wanna be that way, I don't wanna grow up. Seems like folks turn into things that they'd never want; the only thing to live for is to-day-ay!

And then it began to rain. You said you wanted some time alone. "Do you not want me to come over?" I asked, on the edge of disappointment. "No, no, not at all," you said, smiling. You looked at me, the rainfall moving through the late summer air. We were sitting on the steps of the church in the middle of the campus, smelling the fresh air, my head leaned upon your shoulder. When the first drops made their way languidly to our connected bodies, we sat for a bit as if we didn't want it to end, as if we didn't want to be forced away. I had just been looking at the star-filled sky and thinking how lucky I was. Is this a dream, or has life really happened? Have I reached what I had spent so long wishing for in that prison house of my parents' relationship, in that prison house of Coney Island and Brooklyn and Manhattan and New York City, in that prison house of a history destined to end with me, which I had begun to fear would end according to how it began—disappointedly. A disappointed history ending in disappointment. But now here we were, and up there were the stars.

"You're so beautiful," you said, your face melting into love. "I will never not want you not to come over. I just wanted some time alone." You paused and looked at me. I must have looked heartbroken because you pulled me into you and hugged me tight. "Don't worry so much, silly. I'm so in love with you—you have nothing to worry about." Tears had already begun to make their way from my soul to my eyes; and though I was comforted, I couldn't hold back the inevitable first few from descending.

You looked me in the eyes as the rain increased.

"Is that OK?" you asked.

"Yes."

"Are you sure? Because if it's not, come with me now."

The rain began to pound the concrete steps of the church, muddying the grass and gardens of the nighttime campus.

"I'm sure. I'm sorry—I just got nervous."

We stared at each other, unwilling to leave the glance and glare of one another's blue eyes.

"OK. Go—go before we both drown," I said, smiling.

You grabbed me tight. "Oh, thank you! Thank you for understanding! Just an hour."

I love you. I love you too. Your lips are on my lips, the thunder of an ending summer bleeding clear like a slaughter upon the ground. Your tongue and my tongue and our lips, emissaries of love, trying to convey a message as the slaughter falls between the kiss.

I watch as you rush through the mud to Annandale Road. The campus emptied, I stroll back to my trailer comforted in your love.

And then it began to pour.

And then it began to pour.

So we try and try, even if it lasts an hour, with all our might, we'll try and make it ours, 'cause we're on our way, we're on our way to falling in love.

Earlier this morning, he said "I love you." I had only known him for two weeks; and though those two weeks were amazing, was two weeks enough time to fall in love? Spring was here and all the Earth was exploding with everything it had been forced to hold back during the winter. Merissa had dropped me off in

the parking lot next to Olin Hall. I had been debating if I
should go to class or stay in bed with him, but then he
went to class, and I stopped by Merissa's on my way up
to my room, and when she saw me she yelled, "Gorgias."

"Hey."

She mimicked me, "Hey."

She stopped for a second and gave me a long look.
"Were you with your boy all night?" I didn't answer.
"Oooo, someone's in love," she yelled to the other people
in the room. The small room was full and bustling with
activity. "No. No. I'm just kidding," she said, laughing.
She tried to say something else but couldn't, she was
laughing so hard. Klara walked up to me with a smile
and half-shut eyes, and said, "Forgive her. We've been
up all morning smoking pot."

"Oh, my God," Merissa bursted out. "You have to try
this pot! Jason brought it down this morning. It's fucking
amazing!"

"Wait, aren't we going for a drive?" Klara asked.

"Oh, yeah," Merissa said. "OK everyone, we're going
for a drive. Don't steal anything while I'm gone."

"You wanna come?" Klara asked.

"Yeah, sure."

So we went on a drive, and Klara rolled a joint in the
passenger seat, and we took the back roads, and we
passed Poets' Walk, and Merissa said, "Oh, look
Gorgias—Po-*Ets'* Walk."

"Oooo—how romantic! You should go with your new
boyfriend to Po-*Ets'* Walk."

"Can you keep your eyes on the road?" Klara demanded nervously.

"I am."

"No you're not," Klara said, laughing. "Merissa, seriously—keep your eyes on the road! I don't want to die."

I watched the crooked trees along the upriver side of the road. One winter drive, Emily and I had passed these same trees. I had made a joke about them being in a concentration camp for trees; and Emily replied, "I feel as crooked as those trees."

I was thinking about what he said this morning when Klara asked, "When's your next class?" and I remembered that now, now was my next class; and I had one immediately after that across the hall.

"Fuck!" I said.

"What?" Merissa asked.

"It's now."

"That's what I thought," Klara said.

(She was in the next class with me, so she knew that I had a class before that one.)

"It's OK. I can miss this one," I said. Is two weeks enough time to fall in love?

Crooked trees. The smooth road. The sound of paper being licked in the passenger seat.

"Yeah, but Luders will *kill* you if you miss any more of his classes."

"Uggh," Merissa yelled out. "God, can you two please shut up! Who cares? It's springtime and we're eighteen—who cares about this shit?"

140

She took in a breath.

"Hey, Gorgias. Can you find the Neutral Milk Hotel tape."

"Why do you call him Gorgias?" Klara asked.

"GORGI-AAA-S." Merissa yelled out madly. I wonder if she'll turn out to be a psychopathic killer.

"Is it like *Gorgias, Gorgias*?"

"Yeah, she named me Gorgias last summer during Freshman Orientation."

"That's what you guys did for the three weeks of Orientation?"

"That and smoked lots of pot," Merissa said, laughing. "Ganja!"

Klara rolled her eyes. "Guys, take it a little more seriously."

"Uggh, you're so annoying!" Merissa exclaimed. "Did you find that tape yet?"

I find the tape and hand it to Klara. I hear it slip into the tape player. The sound of a lighter igniting follows. *Sinking ship, how long can you hold still, your illness fills this empty room. A portrait of your lover softly drowning in the warm waters of June.*

We didn't say anything else until we hit the diner in Kingston. When we returned to campus, I asked Merissa to drop me off in the Olin parking lot. I was late for Luders's class, but Klara was right—I should go just to stay afloat. Now, walking up the stairs that lead to Olin Hall, I still can't get over what he had said earlier in the morning. "I love you." I didn't answer back. I got scared—because I just can't believe that two weeks is enough time to fall in love. I got scared that he might not be the real thing. I open the doors to Olin Hall and step into the comfort of the temperature-conditioned air.

I lost myself on a cool damp night, gave myself in that misty light, was hypnotized by a strange delight, under a lilac tree.

I had decided to come up early during the winter recess. When the semester had ended—that semester for which I had waited all my life and which had come to me as all my life had come to me—in the stark realities of excruciating disappointment—I watched Emily pack her things haphazardly into her white jeep and then drive away. A hailstorm had started, and I stood in the middle of the empty white campus listening to the frozen ice hit the sidings of our trailer dorm, the paved roads, the mud; I felt the hail hitting my body like bullets.

I was waiting outside in the hail for Erica to get her stuff out of her dorm. She was a freshman, and I was now a sophomore. I didn't care about her; I just needed a ride back to New York. We had lunch with her brother and sister at some diner, and I felt terrible. I had never expected this. I had never expected to be here. I thought this winter would be the best winter of my life. We sat around, uncomfortably poking at omelets and burgers. In the barrage of questions Erica's brother kept asking, all I could think about was where I was supposed to be, where I was certain I would have been—lying right now on your couch, in your arms, staring out at the abandoned pathway of Annandale Road. Maybe a kiss, maybe a tightening of your arms around my body, so that you wouldn't lose me. Maybe not.

"So what do your parents do?" Erica's brother asked me.

Erica jumped in quickly. "He's not... close with his parents."

"Oh, well, you're welcome to stay with us as long as you want."

"Thanks," I said, upset that I might actually have to accept his unsolicited charity.

An armistice in conversation ensued. Mumbled conversations broke through in the cease-fire: some lady claimed to be tired of being a prostitute, and she was convincing her male friend that she'd give the life up just for him as soon as she could; a lone figure kept asking the waitress for more coffee, though his cup was full; parents yelled at children; children yelled at nothing; this all set against the sounds of water flowing into glasses and the scraping of knives against plates.

"My mother's a manicurist, and I don't know about my dad. I don't really have one."

"Oh," Erica's brother said.

Erica throws him a disdainful look. I feel horrible.

143

I thought you'd save me, but you just brought me back home, harder and heavier back to that home, which does not exist.

I stayed at Erica's for a bit, then got my job back at TOYS "R" US. One day, during a break at work, I saw some Goth kids smoking in the parking lot. It was grey outside, and the waters of Caesar's Bay sent a chill across the paved and empty parking lot. I thought of you; I only thought of you, always. The first time I saw you, you were sitting in an empty classroom. You were wearing all black, and my eye caught your left wrist, which was braceleted with various pieces of string. Then I saw the X on your white hand. Your hands were large and white and thin, and you had long bony fingers. I thought you were a little Goth. Later on, I learned you were just dark. The fascinations with vampires and the Cure. Your obsession with Bela Lugosi. It was an innocent darkness, a darkness of things without substance, which, with time, had turned you into a vampire. Inside, you had become a vampire. The innocent darkness of the suburban child had become the real mechanics and devices of a young man who had come of age into darkness, who had finally become. And what he—what you—became was a dark and cold creature.

After work that day, I sat in the park with two tired girls and watched as one of them prepared some tinfoil to freebase a mixture of pot and coke. She offered me some, and I said, "No, thanks." I couldn't do it. I had to go back. So the next day I quit. Two days later—a week

144

left in the winter break—I took the train to Poughkeepsie, and Steve picked me up. You had already come back. So had a lot of other people. I don't think Steve had left. Steve never left.

"So, how was your break?" he asked.

I stared out the window, an anxiety rising in my body and soul. "Good." Lie.

I smiled. Another lie.

A pause.

"How was your break?" I asked, but I didn't care.

"It was fine. I just stayed up here. You know me, I never leave," he said, laughing.

"Why is that—you know—that you never leave?"

"I don't know," he said. "Doesn't seem like there's anywhere to go. Not that I like this place. I hate this place. But I can't think of anything better, so why bother, right?"

While Steve kept talking about all these dumb things, he missed *all three entrances for the campus*. He didn't even *realize* that until I pointed out the sign for Tivoli. "Oh," he said, laughing. "Oops!" On the way back, he entered through the north entrance; and as we drove south to main campus, we passed your house on Annandale Road. I saw some cars parked in the driveway, but the light in your room wasn't on.

"Everybody's back," Steve said.

"Everybody?" I asked.

"Yeah. He came back a week ago."

"Who?" I asked bitterly.

145

There was a pause.

"No one." Steve said. "No one."

Steve was a romantic who loved Tennessee Williams. He too had been in love with you once. He probably still was. The disgusting reality of our relationship definitely disheartened him. It was real, too real to handle.

We sat in silence until we reached my trailer.

"Thanks for the ride."

"Sure," he said. "Hey, listen—there's a party up at the Ranch tonight. You should come."

I looked at him wondering if he was stupid or blind or what.

"Maybe." I said. "See you later, Steve. Thanks again."

"No problem," he said, smiling. "By-eeeee."

I didn't go up to your house that night, and I spent my first day doing everything I could *not* to go up to your house. I picked up a copy of Kierkegaard's *Concluding Unscientific Postscript* and underlined some sentences, but it didn't interest me. I had skimmed most of the work for the class so far. I think I only read *Fear and Trembling*. That was enough for me. The only thing that interested me about Kierkegaard was that he reminded me of a graffiti artist because he always wrote under pseudonyms—that and his idea of a leap of faith. I didn't need to read all the nonsense he ever wrote because I got everything I needed from him already. But then I pictured my mom filing away at the well-known fingernails that held the story of southern Brooklyn's demise. I pictured her back curving more with each day as she waxed the same pubic hairs she had for ten years and manicured the same nails, which disintegrated like clockwork. I pictured her arthritis, her menopause, her migraines, her depressions, her inescapable prison in Coney Island—all to pay for my delusional attendance at Bard College. I imagined how that was the price she paid to earn her doctorate in the bodies of women who history will never recognize, and whose memory time will nullify with the passing of only two generations.

America ignores into invisible her manicurists, schoolteachers; America housekeepers her saints. But these the silent and unseen are like string under the pearls; cut the string, and what was once a necklace comes crashing at the ground.

I tried some more. "Not until the end of it all will everything become clear." Blah, blah, blah, blah. "Oh yes, in the end everything will become clear, but the end is not here yet."

Still grasping my pen, I look up and out the window with its screen of dust and dirt. The snow has begun to fall again. The brown couch below the window—the one we got our first day back—that same day you and I had sat on some shopkeeper's steps in Red Hook—("Is everything OK?", "Something doesn't feel right.")—has been overly stained; and various pairs of dirty jeans and t-shirts and empty potato chip bags, left behind in our collective scramble to leave, are piled on top of it. Sigh.

I turn my head downwards: "the youth," blah, blah, blah, "is rejected," blah, blah, "and has suffered shipwreck," blah, blah, "on his one and only wish." Blah. "What will a person not do for the sake of his one and only wish!" Blah, blah, blah. "How many an entire human life has passed in this way, so that from early youth it has moved incessantly in parenthesis!" I stop and think of Dylan's "Subterranean Homesick Blues"—("get born, keep warm, short pants, romance, learn to dance, get dressed, get blessed, try to be a suck-cess, please her, please him, buy gifts, don't steal, don't lift, twenty years of schoolin' and they put you on the day shift.")

I tried to stay away, but there was nothing to hold me back. The campus was isolated, and the snowfall made the isolation even more biting. I felt something. It wasn't loneliness; it was a feeling of nonexistence, of not being there at all. If I died right now, I thought, no one would know, probably because I'm as good as dead already.

So I did what every desperate dreamer, what every pilgrim must do to feel that he is whole—I went to you, my dream, my idol, my other half. Deep within me growled that great drug of the desperate dreamer—hope; hope that what had rotted and collapsed would resurrect and come back to me. Hope is a privilege only for the innocent. When hope dies, the child dies with it. Adult, person, citizen—all epitaphs to cut into our skin for the slaughtered children coffined deep within.

I walked up the hill to Annandale Road. The trees had icicles hanging from their bare limbs. A car drove by, slowly and cautiously. Besides that, nothing but the sound of my steps on the ground passing the forest to my right, where we had stopped that last day of our freshman year, and you grabbed me and kissed me and then went down on me. I laughed, "What if someone catches us?" "No one will catch us," you say looking up and smiling, "and even if they did—I don't care. I love you." Images and motions sound against our whispers to soft their settle on the spring night dew, which holds nothing outside of me and you; and the newborn leaves provide us cover as you get down onto your knees and place your wetness on mine down below, and no one else could ever know that such a beauty could exist—all that now is passing with the wind that blows from the forest, jingling the icicles and lilting the barren branches into a soft alarm; hitting my heart like an angry ghost: a ghost angry that it is fading into the irretrievable past.

When I saw your house across Annandale Road— that big house on the hill—it seemed full of life. Cars were parked all the way down the curving driveway. I saw you as you passed through the living room, a smile on your face, a drink in your hand. I saw Robert, Jason, and Lila too, but all I really saw was you. I stopped for a bit and stared. I was pulled between anger and love: anger that while I had spent the past day nonexistent, here you were alive and well—full of existence; and love for you—so much love that I didn't want to go in because I knew that your smile would fade into a cold and indecipherable grin as soon as I arrived—breaking me a

149

little more. But I had no choice. I had no fucking choice. Another car drives by, slowing down where Annandale Road curved right beside your house.

I crossed the street, the snowfog made visible up by the lonesome lights along the road: and as I headed up the driveway, I could hear it as clear as I had just heard the icicles jingling when the winter wind had passed through them indifferently; I could hear it with each lonely step I took up the hill to your house—the slow and subtle breaking of my heart.

When I reached your porch, there were two kids outside leaning on the wood railing, smoking. I used to lean on that same railing in the summer in a pair of your jeans, getting lost in what the future held. The screen door squeaks. You come out. You hug me from behind. "You OK?" I turn around. The sun hits your eyes—your beautiful blue calm eyes—as if annunciating an angel. "Yeah, I was just smoking." You stare at me, and then you say, "I've never seen such a beautiful thing, and I never will again." All that is past. All that is hanging from the limbs, edging in casted shadows across the morning horror of my youth.

"Hey, what's up?" one of the kids asks. It was Gabe— tall, harmless, unopinionated Gabe. I always wondered if Gabe ever felt anything. Gabe played an acoustic guitar. You and I had heard him play at Manor House on our last night together. He sang, *"The morning bell, the morning bell, light another candle and release me."* Soon the morning bell would toll. It would continue what the evening bell announced—the slow decomposition of that beautiful dream I had seen personified in your beautiful body, and reified in your love. Soon the morning bell would toll. It would continue the evening bell's proclamation—that the unraveling of my American Dream had started. Morning bell and evening bell would toll, abruptly stopping when I missed the train to Poughkeepsie; and then there would be silence unto death.

"You OK?" I turn around. Subdued a sparkle glints your eyes from the ceiling light above: blue. "Yeah. I was just staring at those roses. Where'd you get them?"

Loaded question.

"Oh, someone brought them by."

Bullet avoided successfully.

"They're... pretty."

Pause.

"How are you doing?" you ask nervously (or am I projecting?)

"I'm fine."

I look away from the roses—at you, more beautiful with each look it seems.

You, you, you. I love that word when it refers to you.

"How 'bout you?" I ask.

"I'm good." You pause. "Did you hear that we're doing the Ramayana this semester?"

"No. What's that?"

"It's a Hindu epic, but some director who's supposed to be really brilliant made it into a play."

"Oh."

"Yeah."

"And we're doing it."

Pause.

"Yeah."

Extra long pause.

"It's really good to see you," you say, taking hold of my hand. "It really is."

Your face lights up, brighter with each glimpse, like yet another sun has been absorbed into your orbit.

"It's really good to see you too, _ Corey _*." '

_ You _* smile. _ I _* smile back, but inside me there's a soft drip, a soft leak, a drip and a drop—the music of my heart bleeding. Someone calls you from the other room. You excuse yourself. I watch you walk away. My heart sings, *"The morning bell, the morning bell, light another candle and release me."*

So the days went by; and as I reappeared each day after day after day after day, spending my time at your house until late in the night, you began to grow colder. I was accustomed to this, and yet it's this that I had feared. Seeing that I still loved you, seeing that you were still my all, you slowly withdrew farther and further. The disappearance followed a usual pattern, which would be repeated with regularity for the next two years, until the time finally came when I let you go, until that time came when I finally realized that you had been gone for so long, and that only a representative of that you that I had loved had been here all along. You were just a broken shadow.

That lonesome week on our frozen campus, in the midwinter recess of our sophomore year, you once again presented your familiar liturgy of disappearance. The liturgy went as follows: *I lost myself on a cool damp night.* First went the touch. *Gave myself in that misty light.* Then went the smile. *Was hypnotized by a strange delight.* Then went the light. *Under a lilac tree.* Then went the person. *I made wine from the lilac tree.* Then came the tyrant. *Put my heart in its recipe.* And the tyrant couldn't love. *It makes me see what I want to see, and be what I want to be.* It was like staring at a star and seeing what the star had been so long ago. *When I think more than I want to think, do things I never should do.* Between me and you lies a distance as great as the darkness of space. *I drink much more than I ought to drink*—we're two lone asterisks—*because it brings me back you*—mimicking lost stars.

(*Piano interlude*)

"The sound of your heartbeat is my favorite sound in the world."

From the speakers Nina Simone cries: "*Lilac wine is sweet and heady, like my love,*"

"Your breathing is my favorite sound in the world."

"*Lilac wine, I feel unsteady—like my love.*"

"Our love will never end."

"*Listen to me, I cannot see clearly.*"

"Our love will never end."

"*Isn't that he coming to me, near—ly—here.*"

Dara's uncle had a house in the middle of the woods. She kept making it really clear to everyone that, "My uncle—he's this really rich gay guy from New York—it makes you *sick*, I swear! Wait till you see this house." Over and over again—always stressing that her uncle, who was "this really rich gay guy from New York (City—of course)—had this house"—and how it all made her sick, while begging us to come and visit her while she watched over it in his absence, and how she'd consider it a huge favor because she couldn't handle "all that corrupt capitalism" alone for too long, like it would rape her values at any moment, or something.

"I mean you need to see this house to believe how disgusting it all is, really."

Dara had created her own major, as Bard had allowed kids to do. She was a Postmodern Literature major with a focus on Marxist and Feminist Literary Deconstruction Theory; so naturally, mostly everything made Dara sick.

We took two cars up to the house. I rode in the same car as you, finding a way to manipulate myself next to you. I could see that this made you unhappy. You still had those long Corey* legs of yours, and naturally there would be no way of avoiding their contacting my body. You shifted positions the whole ride up trying to minimize that contact, but it was hopeless: the car was too small and your Corey* legs too long. You'd have to relinquish some physical ground, so you compensated by staring out the window the whole way up to make sure that our eyes could not meet.

154

The house was some ways out because by the time we reached it, the sun had already begun to set. Someone in our car thought it would be fun to park on the outskirts of the property and sneak up to the house pretending that we were commandos on a secret mission. We veered off the long drive up to the house and left the car on the frozen ground. And so the five of us snuck up to the house, holding our hands up like they were guns positioned for attack, the ground giving us away with its creaks despite our best efforts at caution. Maggie kept laughing at the whole thing, calling it "silly"; and you'd hush her reprimandingly, telling her that if she gave us away she'd be fired from the squad. "Oh, whatever, this is silly. I'm walking up there," she said, giving up. "No," you whispered after her, "You'll give us all away." When she didn't respond, you said, "You leave me no choice." You pointed your imaginary gun at her and fired, yelling, "BANG! BANG! BANG!"

"OK. They definitely heard those shots. We have to rush the place now. Go, Go, Go!" And past Maggie we went, the hard snow below us breaking cacophonously under our frantic run. "You guys are stupid," Maggie said, as we ran past her. "Shut up, you're supposed to be dead," Steve yelled, laughing. Maggie gave him the finger, shouting, "I hate you guys," in the little girl voice she used to formulate her verbal communications with the world.

The house was placed high on a hill: a spacious three-floor cabin styled with a modernist sterility, made medieval by the darkening bare trees that surrounded it for miles. When we reached the house, we had to go underneath an archway, which was made from stone. The large front doors, curved ornately from wood, looked like they had been inspired by a vampire novel. You leaned over and whispered in my ear, "I vant to suck your blood!" Nothing—not a glance, not a word—for three hours. It seemed as if I had vanished; and all of a sudden, the Gothic ambience titillated you, and I reappeared, as if by magic. When you said the word "suck," I felt a torrent of blood rush to my dick. I didn't respond. I just stared at you, caught in a trance. Steve knocked on the two large doors and yelled, "Open up! This is the police!" I heard footsteps rushing to the doors, and when they opened, Dara was standing there with her hand on her chest and a relieved smile on her face: "Oh, my God—you guys just scared the shit out of me!" You pointed your imaginary gun into her face and yelled, "BANG! BANG! BANG!—you're dead!"

"Seriously," Dara said, letting us pass. "That was not cool."

"Why?" Steve asked. "Are you guys doing something illegal here? Are you guys doing drugs?"

Dara rolled her eyes. "Yeah, we're doing drugs, Steve."

"What's this?" he said, pointing to some girl who was smoking a joint. "You *are* doing drugs."

156

"Grow up, Steve! Since when is pot a drug?" Dara said.

She lit a cigarette, then asked absently, "Where's Maggie?"

"Maggie said we were stupid, so she walked here alone."

"You let her walk here alone? You guys *are* stupid!"

Dara stepped outside. I could hear her yelling Maggie's name: Maggie! Maggie!

"This place is amazing!" Gabe said in awe. "Dara, when'd your uncle get this place?"

"She went to look for Maggie," Steve said

The girl offered Steve the joint. He waved her off. "No thanks, I don't need drugs to feel good."

"POT IS NOT A DRUG!" a voice yelled from the other room.

"Oh, God, Margot's here," Steve said. "Great, this'll be fun. Sleepover with the living dead."

"I HEARD THAT, ASSHOLE!" Margot yelled from some unseen place above us.

The ceiling was high and vaulted. The cabin's interior clashed viciously with the exterior. Though the décor complimented the modernist statements of the architectural exterior, the interior's framework was monolithically and purposefully Gothic.

"This place is weird," Steve said, as if reading my thoughts.

"No, *you're* weird," Margot said, descending the stone staircase.

I could hear Dara's voice as it neared the entrance, complaining about some guy in her Derrida class.

"Hey, Margot, why did Dara freak out about us leaving Maggie alone?" I asked as she took her final steps to ground level.

"Oh, the place used to belong to vampires, or some shit like that."

"Vampires?" you asked from the seat you had taken by the window. "Do tell!"

(Sound, the door opens inward.)

"Not vampires, but a blood cult."

(Sound, the wind creeps in.)

"A blood cult?" Steve asked.

(Sound, the birds, the closing door.)

"Yes, Steve. A blood cult. My uncle got the place from some people he knew in the eighties. They used to throw blood-cult parties here."

"Oh, yeah, and what happened to them?" Steve asked.

"Well, the person who owned the place became born-again and wanted to get rid of it."

Dara lit another cigarette.

"So they *were* vampires," the girl with the joint proclaimed. "Cool."

"No, Meghan. Vampires are imaginary. These people were real. They were just over-privileged and depraved maniacs who had way too much money and did sick things with it."

Dara walked over to Meghan, put her cigarette out in Meghan's can of beer, and grabbed the joint from Meghan's fingers.

"You think vampires are imaginary?" you asked from your seat.

"No, Corey*. I *know* vampires are imaginary."

"What if I told you I'm a vampire?" you said.

"OK. You're a vampire. Whatever."

"And you guys just left me in the middle of the woods where the vampires could have sucked out all my Maggie blood."

"THERE ARE NO SUCH THINGS AS VAMPIRES!"

The room went silent. In the silence I could hear the faint sounds of distant thunder and a train screeching against the tracks.

"Chill out, Dara," Margot said, walking over to her and taking control of the joint.

Everyone remained silent, and I couldn't wait for the silence to end because the train's screeching grew louder. It sounded like a subway train that had been forced into an abrupt stop. I heard something collide with the metal. It wasn't possible, but it sounded real, too real. It sounded like the collision of metal thunder smashing against something soft, like flesh.

"I know. Let's hear some music," Margot said.

"Oooo, can we hear some Tori?" Steve pleaded.

"You are *such* a fag!" Margot said.

"You *are* such a fag," Dara agreed.

"Whatever. At least I'm not a bitter pessimistic..."

159

"I know," Margot broke in. "How about I pick out the music?"

"Great. That's settled," Dara said indifferently.

Margot walked over to the CD book lying on the floor, and started flipping through the pages. Dara asked if anyone wanted a tour, and the room cleared out. You stayed in your seat, looking out into the darkness, so I decided to stay too. Steve declined the invitation as well, deciding instead to plop himself onto the black leather couch and flip through an issue of COSMOPOLITAN, which he had picked up from the coffee table. The room was silent once again, except for the occasional flipping of pages—paper pages and plastic pages. I heard the collision again. This time it was clear: the metal thunder was a train; the flesh colliding with it was a body. Then silence, the room again, and I see you: you're staring at me from across the room, a vague smile on your lips.

"I found it! This is what we'll hear tonight, everyone," Margot said happily, waving a CD in her hand.

"*Kid A,*" she said, still flapping the disk in the air. "Hell-o! Ah, forget it."

She walked over to the CD player, the mechanical sound of the disc changer moving, then Thom York's voice: "*The morning bell, the morning bell, light another candle and release me.*"

"I'm not a fag," Steve said, without looking up from his magazine.

"Yes, you are sweetie," Margot replied.

She walked over to the couch and gave him a kiss on the forehead.

"But if you weren't a fag, how the hell would you amuse us?"

"Yeah, because I'm here just for everybody's amusement."

"No, not only you. *Everyone* is here for *everyone's* amusement. Otherwise, we might get bored, or more bored than we all already are."

"Is that even possible?" Steve asked with a weak smile.

"Anything's possible, Stevie. Even being more bored than we all already are."

The stereo speakers continued to chant: *"The morning bell, the morning bell, light another candle and release me."*

We waited for the sunrise in silence.

Lilac wine is sweet and heady—where's my love? Lilac wine —I feel unsteady. Where's my love?

Listen to me—why is everything so hazy? Isn't that he—or am I going cra—zy, dear?...

We were hanging out in my room—me, you, Emily, and Nicole. Jason had left to spend the night at Julie's house, which everyone called the sorority house. The peaceful calm of the collegiate spring has fully overtaken our lives. Nothing will ever change. We don't even think about change, because change is a factor of time; and time, too, has disappeared. It will be like this forever and ever and ever.

I'm leaning against your torso. I imagine your skin under that Tori Amos t-shirt. I imagine that white solid frame and those large pink nipples. I look at you. I can't wait to get to your place. You smile, sensing what I'm thinking, and slip your hand under my shirt. At its touch, my cock bulges, and my nipples get hard. I lean into your ear and speak in a voice overwhelmed by hormones and anticipation. "I can't wait to suck your dick tonight." You smile, and I can feel your body getting hotter.

Nicole was laughing at another pantomime performance Emily was improvising for her amusement. Her laughter grew and grew until it became a cackle.

Tonight, Emily will sleep in my room with Nicole. Your roommate's away, so we'll walk across the dirt path, you and I, to your room. Youthful romance has brought chaos to the living situations of the campus. Your roommate spends his nights in his girlfriend's room; mine has set up camp at his girlfriend's house; and Emily and Nicole stay in my room. I spend my nights with you, in your bed, which is quickly becoming my bed too. All the order of mine and yours and his and hers is collapsing for those who have fallen under the spell that love has cast upon a group of kids in their final months of freshman year.

"What are you guys doing over there?" Nicole asks.

We had started by kissing and got lost. I was

straddling you, and our mouths were sucking each other up, not knowing where to go or what to do. My hand had found its way to your cock, and you had moved it away with much difficulty. "We can't do that here," you whispered, short of breath, sneaking a lick into my ear. You moved my hand behind you, and I dropped it underneath your boxers. I felt your ass burning. I imagined that cock I loved—how hot and full of blood it was, and how my lips would work it for hours as you looked down on me with soft eyes in a dim room.

"You know, there are people here," Nicole said, getting up from the floor.

It took us everything we had to regain control of our lips and unlock them. We stared at each other and smiled, unable to break away from each other's eyes.

"Nicole," I whined, hiding my head in between your shoulder blades.

"No. I mean it. This is quite unacceptable!"

She was kidding, but it was annoying—for everyone. Nicole was the only one in the room who wasn't a sexed-up teenager. She wanted the enjoyment of company; we had had enough of company.

"Let's play a game," Nicole said, clasping her hands.

"Nicole,..." you started.

"He's corrupting you. Look what you've done, you demon spawn—you've corrupted a perfectly good boy!"

Interpol's new song announced itself from the radio speakers, saving the room from silence.

"Come on," she said, struggling to keep a sober face. "Let's play a game!"

"I like this band a lot," Emily said.

"Me too."

"You guys are no fun!" Nicole said, lighting a Camel Light off the cherry of the one she had just been smoking.

She caught Emily's expression, which I could see from my hiding place in between your shoulder blades. Emily's body radiated annoyance and frustration.

"And what's your problem, missy?" she asked.

Emily did not answer.

"Oh fine, I was only joking," Nicole said.

I whispered in your ear that we should go.

"Listen, guys, don't fight.... We're going to go, OK?"

But they didn't care. A small fight had already ensued with Emily complaining that Nicole never wanted to be alone with her, and Nicole saying that she did, that she was only joking, and the same crap they always went through and always ended by rolling around naked on the floor.

We crossed the dirt path to the dorm they had moved you into after they vacated the Hirsch Ravine. We get inside your room. I strip down to my underwear. Your shirt is off. My knees rest on your bare feet. Your cock is in my mouth. I go for it hungrily, and you exhale a sigh of relief. We move to your bed, and now my ass is rubbing against your cock, and I get lost in the kisses and the sweating and the coming. I get lost in us over and over again. We try to sleep a bit as the light approaches, but we can't. No matter how much we come, our cocks get hard, and we end up fooling around until we've come so much that we can take a rest and enjoy holding each other.

We don't leave your bed for hours, maybe days. Time does not exist for lovers. We just suck and kiss and grab and sweat and rest and suck and kiss and sweat and wrestle. We run out of water, and you put on a pair of sweatpants to get stocked up at the vending machine. While you're gone, I discard the sheet, and lie flat under the room's soft light.

I hear the cautious opening of the door. I hear your mesmerized voice say, "Wow." I hear the material of your sweatpants folding down your legs. You get on top of me and gyrate your cock. I try to force it in, but you stop me.

"Why?" I ask, turning around. "Don't you want to lose it to me?"

You pause to take a breath. "It takes everything I have to wait."

"Why do you want to wait?"

"Because," you say, turning me over, grabbing hold of my hands, your beautiful face hovering over me. "I don't want to lose it in some dorm room we'll never see again. I want the place to be special. I want it to be ours."

I smiled. Our lips moved forward. We kissed with open eyes.

So, we waited a month until we found that special place, and we almost lost it in your new house on Annandale Road in that summer of our love. But it didn't work. I got scared that I might bleed and have to go to the hospital and fucked it up. The first time was your fault, the second time was mine, but we almost missed out on the greatest spiritual experience of our youth.

We finally fucked two weeks before we ended; and even under the weight of our crumbling love, we couldn't get enough. Had we but let ourselves be free to seize the original moment, which had presented itself twice in the heyday of our love, I think that we both would have left unbroken once the relationship had ended. Everything we had ever dreamed of—all that sexual anxiety and emotional pain that had built up in the repression of our teenage years—finally had a chance to be settled. Those two actual moments don't matter in themselves; their importance lies in how they symbolize the neglect, the disdain, and the indifference that we both showed to a gift so rarely granted—the gift of true love.

The Universe had presented us a tender dove. We left it in the storm to wither away and die.

At night I wake up with the sheets soaking wet, and a freight train running through the middle of my head, only you...

Two weeks ago, I told you everything—everything that I had been hiding for so long.

I had said that I had something important to say, but that I needed time to get the courage to say it; and then you called the trailer this morning and asked me to come over. "Great," I said, "I'm ready to tell you." There was a silence over the receiver. "Tell me what?" A pause. "That thing I tried to tell you last night but wasn't ready. Well, now I'm ready to tell you."

We went up to your room, and you mentioned that something was on your mind.

"What is it?" I asked.

You asked that I go first. "I want to hear what's so important."

I got nervous, but then I remembered what Emily told me a few days before we returned for our sophomore year. It was the night before we made our last trip to Smith Point for the summer. I cried the whole night. Emily held me. I told her everything, and I told her how scared I was to tell you. She said that you'll accept me because you love me, just as she had done.

So I told you.

I told you about my mother, and how I cry about her life, and how pathetic I felt that I neglected her. I told you about how my father had chased me out of the house with a knife a month before I went up to Bard for my freshman year. I told you about how poor we were, and how I had always felt different; not an immigrant, but not an American; neither a street kid nor a child of suburbia. I told you how I had felt lost for so long; and how bad it hurt to be one thing on the inside, and watch helplessly as every moment the inside truth clashed violently with the truth of the outside. I told you how I stopped us from having sex that time in your new house because I was scared that I might bleed badly and have to go to the hospital, and how then you'd see that I had no medical insurance. I told you who I really was—as far as I knew myself to be—and I thought that it *would* be fine because Emily *promised* me that it would be fine; and by the time I finished, I needed you to hold me. I needed you to comfort me.

You sat close by without touching me. You were silent until my crying calmed.

Then, in a cool flat voice, you said, "We just aren't working anymore."

Your statement shocked me—I was so hooked to you that I didn't even consider what had just happened to ever even be a possibility. I begged you to talk it over. You agreed. We talked it over. By the end, we were kissing. It was on that night we finally fucked.

A remembrance of virginity lost: You slid in. Where there had once been pain, there was now only pleasure. It fit perfectly, now that all the anxiety was gone. It fit perfectly now, as that which had been he for so long finally completed its transformation and became you. I watched your eyes above mine as you moved with care and caution in and out; and I felt it. I felt love. We came at the same time, and you kissed me, and you told me that you would love me forever so, "don't worry, OK?", "OK."

We lasted two more weeks. I would say that those days were filled with making love; but the time for such language had passed us. We fucked a lot—and it was great—but it was really nothing more than fucking. We fucked to drown out the noise of our love collapsing.

It is now our last night together. I'm lying on my back in your bed in the room I had told you to steal away from Maggie. Your back is to me. The clock says 8:46 AM. I look at your back. I have an urge to touch you.

I lay my hand on your shoulder, which is lit from the porch light below, and the window is open, and you turn your head to me, and I smile, and I lower my arm, lower, and lower, and my hand begins to stroke your hard cock, and you stare at me with vacant eyes. You are lying there like a corpse with a hard-on. Your cock is stiff, but your love is gone.

I sigh and turn away, and I know your eyes are open, and I begin to cry, and then you get up and say, "I can't do this anymore." And I beg and beg and beg and beg, but you keep saying, "It's over."

Your vacant eyes fill with tears. Stray cold rays from the porch light below hit them, and I see your eyes sparkle like stars for the last time.

The last of the summer night air comes through the window. The red light digits of your alarm clock announce that it's 9:03 PM. We're looking into each other's eyes. We're holding hands. I feel your long bony

169

fingers, your Corey* fingers, the fingers I love so much, and I begin to wail; and you start crying, too. You try to reassure me that we'll be OK. I ask you how can we be anything when we are ending? You don't have an answer, and I know that it has ended. I know that all this that I love—the long Corey* legs, the Corey* blue eyes, the Corey* place between your shoulder blades where my head fit perfectly, and which you told me was my safest place on Earth—I know that all this is now gone. No more private jokes that only we could understand. No more beautiful cock in the morning. No more your eyes colored by the setting sun at Blithewood Garden. Simply, no more you.

All those dreams I wished upon my childhood stars are slipping away like sandcastles in a nightstorm might slip—and when he awakes, the child wonders where his castles went—into the ocean's waters—and who it was that swallowed up all the sand. I look out the window and I see the summer trees, and I begin to let go of your hand, finger by finger, knowing that us holding hands is all that we have left. I release your hand. Offering no resistance, it limply falls away. I dress slowly. I leave calmly. I don't say good-bye.

I take a moment on Annandale Road and look up at your window. I had hoped you might be looking through it, but the curtains are drawn. I imagine your body splayed on the large mattress. I imagine you staring at the ceiling, whispering chants and death hymns to remove the weakness that loving me had made you feel.

Somewhere, a boy is spending his night crying in the arms of a girl named Emily. That boy is me.

Somewhere, a boy is lying supine on his back, staring at his ceiling and killing what was beautiful in him. That boy is you.

Somewhere, a boy is crumbling; and all that he had fought so long to keep from showing breaks through and destroys him.

Somewhere, a boy is telling himself to be strong and to be cold and to be ruthless and to have purpose and to grow up and to gain power, and he is freezing over.

He is freezing.

I am melting.

That night, you froze. That night, I burned.

I looked past the platform at Manhattan's skyline. The Empire State Building peeked out in a peaceful obstinacy to make its presence known. Once again, New York had gone without a night. What time is it? "9:03," someone had said. The banging of the metal cars breaks in, the grey pavement, the grey sky, the greyed grey world. A voice is born from the thunder and the clash of the metal train. I only hear the voice of the thunder and the clash. It breaks through to me, and look—here's the skyline, and look—there's the train, and look—your eyes in the window; and I hear it, the thunder and the clash— and the wind sluices around the curves of my downfalling body.

Lonely is the room, the bed is made, the open window lets the rain in. Burning in the corner is the only one who dreams he had you with him.

You made me a mix-tape, which you sent in a large box filled with letters you had written for me on your trip that summer through Italy. My mother was in the kitchen scrubbing the spotless tiles of the floor when the package arrived. Instead of joy, the box on my mother's kitchen table made me feel malice. It was one month into our summer vacation. By now, the boy from Bard had crumbled under the reality of his life in Coney Island.

Before you left for Italy, I had made a trip to Boston. The semester had ended only two weeks ago, and I was still the happy boy you knew. We went to some club called ManRay with your best friend from high school. Her name was Molly. All we did the whole time was stare at each other. I saw beautiful boys in the periphery, and felt the tension with which I later became so familiar: that tension of desire and hope scratching the walls from the drugged and drunk eyes of the lonely and the lost children of the night; but nothing could pull me from that gaze, which was your gaze; and then we walked through the quiet summer streets of Boston; and when Molly left to go to work in the morning, we fooled around; and when Molly came back from work earlier than we had expected, she caught us naked; and then we ate breakfast; and then the train waited for me at the station.

You watched me from the platform as I boarded the train. You watched me as you would do so many times from so many platforms, you watched me as my train left; and I watched you as I would do so many times out of so many train windows, I watched as he receded into yet another irretrievable moment; and even in my happiness, the worry was there—that this moment ended meant that one day all moments might follow.

Years later, I found one of those long Italian letters in a cigar box I used for storage. I had hidden it in an attempt to erase you from my life. The pearl-colored papers lay at the bottom of the box underneath the lilac blossoms you had picked for me on one of our last days of freshman year, and the silver penguin figurine you had sent with your letters from Italy.

(Though long dead, the lilacs continued to exude a potent scent.)

I removed the letter from its exile, then noticed another object—it was the cross you had bought for me when I came to visit you in Boston. You had the jeweler inscribe "God's Peace" on the cross. When I asked why you chose "God's Peace," you said, "Because that's what my name means. Corey* means 'God's Peace.'"

I unfolded the letter's multiple pearl papers. It read:

Italy—letter one

TO _____*
WITH LOVE
FROM AN
INCOHERENT
COREY*

June 3, 2000
8:46 PM

Dearest _____*,
I'M currently in the air over Cape Cod—the sunset is brilliant from above the clouds. I can think only of you. I'm sorry I couldn't get something out to you sooner—the day was more hectic than planned. I had some small things I wanted to send you, but no letter to accompany them, and now is the first time I've had to write.

This flight has been madness, I tell you, mAdness! I think David Bowie is my flight attendant. I'm drinking AiR ItaLia wine—the logo on the twist-off-cap bottle assures quality. At any random point I may have to stop writing—I've overheard the plans of the Italian elderly gentleman in front of me to put his seat back, which will incapacitate me completely—

planes were not built for
people with long, Corey* legs.
so if I stop mid-sentence...

I'm really trying to write legibly for you. I hope I am... Oh, a warning about this paper. Most pages

174

contain a random quote on the subject of love—they do not necessarily refer to our relationship. I don't want you thinking I'm choosing spiteful stationary or anything. It's just from a journal. You've been warned.

Thank you so much again for coming to Boston. It saved Italy for me—the trip will now be enjoyable. Those hours I spent lying with you will certainly go down as some of the most valuable I've ever had. The images of you coming off the train and the first embrace will forever hold a place in my memory. Sorry the trip home had to be so stressful...

I miss you. Please know that I'm thinking about you.

I think I'm going to read and try to sleep a bit. We'll be arriving 9:03 AM local time.

GRUNT. I CAN'T SLEEP AND I'M DRUNK OFF OF AIRPLANE WINE. The smell of airplane food awoke me, and they turned the lights up to make sure no one would miss the mystery meat rolling their way. I just started listening to your mix tape. I brought only that and my new copy of Gould playing the Goldberg Variations (Bach). Oh—the meal is arriving. Apparently beef or fish...

Well, that was interesting! The attendant couldn't understand my English, so I took the fish (w/lasagna that was basically a cube of pasta with a milk center). There was nothing else but bread, and, sitting w/only wine and bread, I felt a bit like a monk. A few glasses of wine later, I just said, "Well, if you're not going to feed

my vegetarian self, I might as well DRINK my dinner!!!"
The wine just keeps on coming... I must be the resident
lush!

This is a fantastic mix tape... ███████ They're
showing this very strange Italian show that's just people
playing very cruel tricks on each other, a reaction
comedy. Like Candid Camera, only a bit more malicious.
They were just dragging a dummy from under a moving
car—a little woman about 80 yrs old was screaming at
the top of her lungs and chasing after the car, waving her
arms and trying desperately to catch up. Around the
fourth glass of wine this became very amusing...
████████████████████████

I'm already planning my mix tape for you. I think I'll
make you a CD as well, just so it doesn't seem like a
polite response...

Well, however many glasses of wine later, I'm not
sure how my writing is. So, I'm going to try to rest again.
It should work this time, so the next installment should
be from Italy. Maybe a different letter. Just in case....

Missing you. Love, Corey*

Well that didn't work... Its about 1/2 hr later. Its
about 9PM/10PM our time, and it's far too early for me
to sleep, but it's about 4/5 AM Italian time so I really
should. I've had too much wine to read very well, so here
I am again.

They were just showing footage of kangaroos on the
TV for about 17 minutes. I wonder what that was
about.... About 4 more hours to this flight, then Madrid,

no Milan (very different) for an hour, then another flight onward to Venice.

██████████████████████████

This can't be an interesting letter. I should probably stop until I have more to say. I'm just restless, and I don't know what to do with myself. Pretending to talk to you seems like the best option. Maybe you're happy to hear from me in any form. I know I'd do anything to hear your voice right now. I can imagine later...

6-4-00
About 8:46 AM
Italian time

A few hours later, I'm the only one on the plane who seems to be awake. There's a movie playing that seems to be about Meg Ryan talking on the phone... I'm really worried that this is too play-by-play, so I'll take the rising Italian sun as a hint to conclude the letter now.

You mean more to me than anyone right now. I know we say it's impossible, but I hope to show you exactly how much you mean to me. (Don't ask me how I plan to do this. I'm working on it...) I am more thankful for meeting you than any other event in my life right now. Thinking of you...

████████████

I love you.
Corey*

<THE P.S. LETTER>

All right. This concluding thing isn't working out.

It's about an hour later, and I still can't sleep. ██████████████████████████████████ Hey! I've developed a strange facial tic! It started this morning. It's on the curve of my upper cheek that arches up to my nose—very random spot. I think I've had all the fun I can with it though. ███████████████████ I occupied myself for a bit with some Scientology packets. That "Introduction to Scientology" was amazing. We really should have left the instant we saw the red screening room. We've been trained badly. I think I'll take the personality test in the Milan airport. We're about to fly over France...

...so.....tired...................

You're
beautiful.
███████████

I love you!
We'll see each other sooner than it seems.
and the next letter will have
more consistency, after I experience
some stories to tell.
███████████

I'll send the next letter as soon
as possible. Until then...

When you returned from Italy, you moved into the house on Annandale Road, that special place for which we both had waited. I took the train to Poughkeepsie; and the whole ride up, an expectant boy sat by the window and tried to enjoy the beauty of all that which surrounds the river, but he couldn't calm himself—not with the beauty of the river, not with the hillsides he had grown to know so well—so he tried to fasten his attention to something new in hopes that it would help him quiet, and becoming aware of the disintegrating ticket in his sweaty hand, he looked it over: it read, TRAIN TO POKIPSE; and I spent my whole ride up to you trying to figure out why Poughkeepsie was so needlessly misspelled, and that word—POKIPSE—saved me from going insane with desire for the fulfillment that awaited me at the end of the line.

POKIPSE stilled the stir of the fire and lulled the lantern to a glint; that seemingly meaningless misspelling forged a new word, whose discharge captured the attention of a young boy and calmed the passion that was whirling in his thoughts of love as he rushed northward to the one that made that love possible—to his arms, to his feet, to his lips, to his eyes, to his cheeks.

POKIPSE stayed me so that I could get to you; and once there, you and I could disappear into us, and the whole world, with its wars and liars and problems and pain, would just tumbledown away. Through our love, we would sidestep back to the innocence of childhood. Through our love, we would sidestep the distance home.

Even when you were here, you were just an escape from the harsh realities of growing up.

Even when you were here, I was already heading nowhere.

Only cowards fall in love the way you and I had done.

Only fools treat love the way you and I had done.

We used each other, and we used our love; and that not only harmed us, it added to the cripple of those ideals that have been the hallmarks of the human race— lessening Love; gaudying God; diminishing the daylight of Democracy; absolving Art into its arson.

We were never more than the terminal thrash of matches at extinguish.

The sad thing is our story's not unique. It won't become a cherished chronicle of love in the age of double zeros; it's just one of many versions of one short story, which in two sentences expresses the essence of our generation.

This is the only story you need to hear to understand American youth in the age of double zeros.

This is the only story you need to know to find out who we, the flatliners, are:

In the morning we all were children.

By night's arrival, we had slaughtered one another's child.

I hope all is well with you. I wish the best for you. When no one is around love will always love you.

LORIMER-ST. A flat ding and a flat dong. I get up and walk really fast toward the ramp, not even remembering to hope that I won't run into anyone. I hear my name.

"_____," "_____"

Someone's walking toward me. A boy is walking toward me. Steve is walking toward me.

"What, are you deaf?" he says. "I yelled out your name like five times!"

"Steve?"

"Yeah," he says—more seriously, "Are you OK?"

"No. Yes. I'm tired. I had a long night."

"You look really fucked up."

"It doesn't matter—how are you? Are you living in Williamsburg?"

"Yeah," he says, a smile no longer on his face.

"Really? Who are you living with?"

"Maggie and a bunch of people."

"Maggie?"

"Yeah. Everybody's living here."

"Everybody?"

He pauses.

He very obviously wants to get away.

"Yes. Everybody."

He pauses.

And then:

181

"Corey too."

At his name, I smiled brokenly. Steve said he had to go, adding that I should really lay off the drugs. I didn't answer, and he walked away. Your name hit me flat. I have become flatlined. I am a flatliner. Suddenly, I'm on the G train staring at an ad that tells me I should remember to get tested for AIDS. The guy in the ad looks really healthy and has a big smile, and all I can think is, "What the hell does this guy know about AIDS, unless there's a new AIDS, an AIDS of flatness—then this guy must be an expert!"

And the train roars—BROADWAY, FLUSHING AVE., CARROLL ST., Smith-9 Streets.

Jack's voice comes in from the other end of the line forming these words: "Are you OK?" I pause. Beth has wandered in from the women's side of the ward. I watch her as she heads toward me, her slippers rubbing against the floor, a mischievous smile curved on her lips. "Am I OK?" I think, a soft smile breaking on my lips in response to Beth, who's pretending to be sneaky. Am I OK?

It's been seven months since I went back into the Coney Island Hospital ER, my legs missing, my body broken, my voice soft and weak. I had walked on a frozen lake with Emily, somewhere on the outskirts of Port Jefferson. I remembered her face that night as she stared at the painting of Lisa while she snorted herself away. I remembered her face as they carted me on my back through the halls, the lights above hanging like alien ships uncertain whether they should land, interrupting my memories of my friend with—each—passing—light. Lisa had come back to torture her like an old addiction; and no magic whisper—neither wind nor prayer—could help Emily make the stalking ghost disappear.

> There was no more morning light,
> Except the beams approaching Smith-9
> Streets station.

Emily died that night—or morning. It was hard to tell, because we had been up for days doing coke. Now it seems so long ago. I spent the week at her house, and everyone moved around in a silent numbness wondering who it was that we could blame. I feared that it was going to be me; that I'd end up the one who was at fault, because I was the one who watched her as her breathing grew heavy; and I was the one who felt her as she broke into a sweat; and I was the one who asked if she was sick; and when she said, "No. I'm fine," I was the one who figured that she was fine, and I was just being paranoid because of the coke, so I went to bed; and when I woke up, she wasn't breathing; and I was the one who shook her; and having no idea where to go or what to do, I was the one who just sat by her and kept doing line after line after line until her mother came home and walked into the room full of life; and there I was, huddled in the corner with the white residued mirror and Emily dead and cold beside me; and I looked up at Nancy, and she knew, and she yelled, and she cried, and it seems like she never stopped crying. And I was the one who should have known better; but I was too numb; and after the initial anger would come the understanding; and I knew that I was the one that we would blame.

For one week, we walked around like flickering shadows. No one said a word. One morning, I woke up and saw Nancy standing over me. "I'll drive you to the train station," she said. And I knew who was to blame.

Was I OK? No—I wasn't. I was doomed; and watching Beth come to me, I felt that I was destined to share her fate—alone and old, tucked away in some mental ward where I would be left to die a nothing. I was just about to try and say all that to Jack—the smile on my lips grown larger—when his voice broke in through the receiver once again, and I heard, "It's such—it's a miracle you survived. After you're released, I'd like you to come and stay with me." Hearing that, I began to cry. Beth stopped and started to yell and cry really loud, mimicking me. All I could hear was Beth yelling, crying, "Nobody wants me! Nobody wants me!" They came to take her away, and she fought. I watched her recede— through the pools in my eyes—and all I could hear was the madness in her voice as she vanished, her voice still crying, "What am I going to do? What am I going to do?"

They left me to my crying, because Beth was too big a

problem: the nothing was showing that it was a something still; and still, I hear her, "What am I going to do?"; and still, I see Nancy's face as she sees her daughter dead, and me with wide black eyes moving from the shaky mirror, up to her, Nancy, and then me saying, "I think Emily's dead," and she is. She, Emily, is dead.

After I got off the phone with Jack, I wheeled myself into my room. Through the gated windows, I saw cars heading south and north along OCEAN PKWY. It was a pretty day, and I figured that people were trying to get one last day in at the beach. The papers had been reporting that this was to be the last season that the amusement park would be up, having been bought out by a realtor. This would be the first serious move of gentrification into one of New York's last untouched places. I pushed the blanket off of what was left of my legs. There were no more rides, no more days at the beach left for me.

I went over to a box that my mother had brought over. It was where I had kept all the things that fell out of the sky to make up my life. Its contents consisted of dead lilacs, a silver penguin figurine, a cross that pronounced "God's Peace," Corey's letters, some black and white pictures of me and Josh taken in a photo booth, a crumpled train ticket dating back to August 2000 with the words TRAIN TO POKIPSE, and something that was just recently returned to me—a blue letter in a blue envelope.

I opened it and read it only for the second time:

I thought about the advice that you gave me this morning when we walked on the frozen lake. I know that I agreed to take it but I just can't let my heart go into hiding. I just can't let myself be an expatriate from the only thing that matters in life which I know you also know is love. I DO remember that time we went to Smith Point. I'm sorry I didn't tell you and if it hurt your feelings but please know that I do remember. It was the day after you told me about your parents and your life. I remember the night before much more than that day at the beach but I know that you like to remember only happy meaningless moments because it seems you've had so few happy meaningless moments in your life.

We were watching videos on YouTube of Blind Melon and Nirvana and we were talking about how Shannon Hoon died at twenty-eight and Kurt Cobain died at twenty-seven. We wondered why all that magic disappeared and if it would ever come back and then you told me you have something important to say. It seemed serious but I didn't know what it could be. I knew you were with Corey and I knew that he was your first so it couldn't be AIDS or something serious like that but you started crying and I ran to you and I held you. You told me that you never told this to any one before. You told me that you were scared and that the worst response a

186

person could give was a noncommittal one (you said something like "I don't want anyone to react to me like I'm just another television show") but I reminded you that I was your friend and asked no begged to hear it.

"My dad chased me out of the house with a knife two weeks before I came to Bard. My parents are poor, and I hate them, and I hate myself, and I'm so embarrassed to be who I am." I didn't respond immediately because I was shocked. You did such a good job at hiding it. I mean I and most everyone thought that you were from privilege just because that's how you presented yourself. But that didn't matter to me. Only you mattered to me. I held you and you cried the whole night. We talked it through and you told me that you wanted to tell Corey. I said that you should. You told me that you were worried about his response and I said that you shouldn't worry because didn't I just prove that "television-show-fear" wrong? Didn't I love you and hold you and accept you and since he loved you wouldn't he do the same and yes you said yes he will yes.

It didn't work out that way with Corey but I had no way to know. I hope you don't blame me for his response but you probably do because you seem to blame the world for everything. Please know that I've always loved you. Please know that I have always been your friend. Please know that it wasn't my fault.

Last night I had two dreams or maybe they were visions.

In the first one I was in a boxing ring and my opponent was Lisa. As I stared at her face it changed. I was more mesmerized than frightened. I stood there watching my opponent become every girl I've ever loved punching me to the ground. My instinct told me to get up but then I realized it wouldn't change. I would just be stuck in that ring forever. So I stayed down while the referee counted "One... Two... Three... Four..."

In the second dream two sailboats were floating in the harbor. One of the sailboats didn't have its sails up. It wasn't going anywhere. The other one raised its sails and was moving and I was on it. I looked up and I noticed that someone had shot all the stars out of the nighttime sky.

Once upon a time in a place far away we were children. I want to go back to that place. I want to go back home.

Emily

I folded the letter.
I closed my eyes.

The G line is not one of New York's famous train lines. When you watch movies from the seventies and eighties you don't ever see a G train passing through the screen, threatening to murder you in the safety of your little cave dwelling. Even on New York

City subway maps, it's the only train line that doesn't have its own color, having borrowed the sharp green of the 4-5-6 and muted it as if to show its own lack of consequence. The G line passes through none of the major train stations of New York. There is no Grand Central or Penn Station; there is no 42 St or 14 St. It has no Coney Island to start at and no Coney Island with which to end. Of all the train lines in New York, the G line is the one that is most lost. It is the nowhither of New York's subway system.

At Smith 9 Sts station the G line ends. The F train stops through Smith 9 Sts, sharing the tracks with the G, but the station is just a footnote along the way of the F train's more significant journey, which ends at Coney Island after a long voyage through QUEENS, MANHATTAN, BROOKLYN.

I had thought about all this as I stared at the map at METROPOLITAN AVE. I had just seen Steve and he told me that you were here, you had been the whole time. Even if I had made it to Poughkeepsie, Emily's letter was right.

"Corey's here. We're all here," Steve had said. That morning journey at recapturing my loss was destined to fail.

Like all that which is neglected, the G line is burdened with a tremendous significance: a significance of space. I had never gone farther than its last stop in Brooklyn at Greenpoint Av; but looking at the subway map as the G train heads to Smith 9 Sts, I noticed all that undiscovered country, all that land hinting at its own galaxy of stories, which whisper humbly into QUEENS and then disappear unmapped, as if there were another world outside of here toward which the human story goes. The whole morning I had been lost in fragmented recollections of my life. I was terrified by the realization of what I had become.

The train stops passed me by: BROADWAY, FLUSHING AVE., Bedford-Nostrand Avs, CLASSON AVE.,...

An ad caught my eyes. Two smiling cardboard representations meant to be human beings looked directly at me. Everyone on the train was just a colored shadow; but these two faces were so clear, like they're the only real things left. Behind them white letters announced, "GET TESTED! AIDS is on the rise."

AIDS. I reflected on the acronym just as I had once reflected on the word POKIPSE. "What are you without your body?" I overheard some yuppie say philosophically as I was bringing her another glass of *pinot noir* during my waiter days. "Thank You. Nothing. Our bodies are all we have."

There was a plague that had frightened the race of man into an acute awareness of his body. It exposed the frailties and the realities of a physical existence. What had started as a fight for survival has altered into a myopic view of existence where your body is the primary concern, and the results of banishing the mind and exiling the soul for the autocracy of the body have begun

190

to poison their way out into our fair American paradise. I thought about everyone my age and saw their faces filled with struggle and a sense of impotence. I thought about my most educated generation, handed a crippling amount of promissory debt for diplomas; then placed behind a counter to pour the miracle martini or by a café table to take an order for no-bean-vegan-cassoulet, Rimbaud's refrains and Plato's musings now only pricking the failure of our role in the American dream, ever harsher, ever further in.

The plague that haunts this generation is another form of AIDS. This disease is the devouring and weakening of the soul. What are you without a body? Well, what are you without a soul? A healthy body, flawless and perfect in its curves with clean skin that's been smoothed by beauty products, and yet, there is nothing inside but a soft scratching. What are you without a body? I don't know, I thought, looking at the large ad with its smiling picturesque faces telling me to "GET TESTED!"; I don't know what you are without a body, but I do know that without a soul you're just another television show.

There was a plague that had frightened the race of man into an acute awareness of his body. They named it AIDS. Twenty years later, a new AIDS stalks us: an AIDS of the soul.

BERGEN ST., CARROLL ST.,...

I am falling.

I am falling.

The light breaks through the perfect sky like an avalanche of hail-fire in a storm, revealing graffiti as we OPEN rise YOUR and rise EYES! and rise—and then the panoramic glory that the G train provides NO MORE CORPORATE BULLSHIT! as it heads in a curve FUK WALL ST. to Smith-9 Streets station, Brooklyn below us low, Manhattan above us high, the water of the Gowanus Canal gluttoned with stilled indifference underneath. In the light, it seems so dead. This beautiful morning light heightens how much America has fallen. It shines without its promise across a land of the fatigued who are dreaming of another time and spirit. That time and that spirit are dead; their memory now haunts the dreams of kids my age with that nostalgia for something we never had. For New York. For San Francisco. For America. The morning light revealed, the darkness of death.

We are the first generation of Americans who are not American. America rests on no values. It defines itself on no precepts. America is and always was dependent on its definition by its frontiers—those dark zones yet to be explored. That's what's always made America a land of possibility—the promise of somewhere else, some wilderness still, where a person can go and make himself anew; the *ability* to imagine such a place, to imagine it so much that it actually becomes real.

I had learned about these frontiers in my high school history class. Most of us learned about these frontiers—that Wild West—conquered and subdued by the twenties, in the boring rooms of high school history class.

Yet even without a Wild West, America lived on. She even flourished, with all the chaotic elements that come with a real flourishing, a real becoming. She lived on because her frontiers had not died, they had just moved. After the Wild West was won, the places of possibility moved to America's cities. There a person could go and begin a new life, just as he could once have done in the Wild West.

America is no more because her cities are no more. It is gentrification that killed America's cities. It is the gentrification of the mind that has killed America for my generation. Those dreams set forth by Ronald Reagan in his Second Inaugural Address when he promised to restate *our values of faith, family, work, and neighborhood* have been realized. A new America has been created—an America without frontiers. The results of that creation are best seen in my generation—a generation of flatliners, a generation of Columbines, a Generation Nothing.

We are the first generation of Americans who are not American. We began somewhere; and though we ended up nowhere, we will always strive to get back to where we should have been—back to our own promised lands. America has raised a slaughtered generation, and we are that slaughtered generation. We are crippled children trying to find our way back home.

It was a beautiful morning. The platform at SMITH 9TH ST. was mostly empty. When the F train came, I knew that I must go home. I used to think that home was an end, a place you go when the day is done; but home,

193

like America, like Love, like God, is a journey of striving toward humanity.

It was a beautiful morning with a clear blue sky.

The platform at SMITH 9TH ST. was mostly empty.

Someone asked for the time. "9:03," someone replied. And...

David and I were on the L train going into the city. And...

There was a boy. And...

There was a dream. And...

There was a city. And...

I was standing on the edge....

And I heard the clattering, the thunder and the clash of the train, and I saw two light beams approaching, and then I looked at her. A shadow city. A shadow America. A shadow dream. And I took out a bag of coke and opened it, but the wind dispersed it into a snowfall, and somewhere in my life the snow is falling, and watching it I realized we are separate snowflakes. We are no longer part of the storm.

I stepped off the platform.

Somewhere in my life, the snow is falling; and it is the snowfall of everything I've been and everyone I've known uniting into a storm.

I am falling,

I am falling,

The tracks approach,

the street below,

9:03,

morning horror,
the metal thunder and the metal crash.
I am falling.
I am falling.
No one can understand how robbed we felt who is
not one of us.
I am falling.
I am falling.
Once upon a time, in a place far away, we were
children.
I am falling.
I am falling.
I am falling home.